PIROUETTE

PIROUETTE

A Novella

E. J. Quigley

iUniverse, Inc.
Bloomington

PIROUETTE
A Novella

iUniverse books may be ordered through booksellers or by contacting:

iUniverse
1663 Liberty Drive
Bloomington, IN 47403
www.iuniverse.com
1-800-Authors (1-800-288-4677)

ISBN: 978-1-4620-4066-7 (sc)
ISBN: 978-1-4620-4067-4 (e)

Printed in the United States of America

iUniverse rev. date: 08/10/2011

Credits

Proofreading and formatting: Geoffrey D. Stone geoffreydstone@gmail.com

Cover Photograph: Barney Leonard barney@blendedmedia.net

Cover design: Saul Rosenbaum: saul@visualchutzpah.com

Pointe shoes courtesy of Jane Lopoten School of Dance *janelopotendance.com*

As a child, I knew that I had one great possession: my body. It was little and quick. I lived within it. I looked out of it with my eyes, my irises, and that was also my name, Iris—like the flower. ... All we actually have is our body ... to glide in the water, to roll down a hill ... to jump into someone's arms.
— From *Once a Dancer: An Autobiography*
by Allegra Kent

Vladimir Petrovsky sat up on the edge of his bed. He lifted a crimson tulip from the vase on his bedside table, pinched the flower from its stem, plucked its petals and spread them softly one by one on the palm of his hand. He imagined that his hand was a pink satin futon and the petals were fragile, beautiful beings, sleeping beauties. They were so light, so soft that he could barely feel them. When he had the petals arranged to his satisfaction, he stroked them one by one drawing his finger along the softness of their edges, hardly touching them, hovering his long index finger over them as seabirds hover over the undulations of a dead calm sea.

Now he began to close his hand slowly. Once it was closed, he flexed the muscles in his forearm, tightening his grip, squeezing down until his fingers turned pale. Then he relaxed his grip and opened his hand. There were damp red stains in the wrinkles of his palm and under his fingernails. He turned his hand palm downward and spilled the crumpled petals on the floor. Then he wiped the red stains away with a linen handkerchief taken and returned to the drawer in his bedside table.

This morning, as she did every morning before Vladimir awoke, Mrs. Petrovsky placed the flower vase on his bedside table. This morning she had filled it with those crimson tulips. Beside the vase she laid a blush-red bachelor's button with a long, slender stem. "There now, my darling," she had whispered to his sleeping ears as she reached down to push a strand of hair the color of lemon custard back from his forehead. Over her arm she had carried a white Egyptian cotton shirt, still warm from the iron. On her way out of his bedroom, she had laid the shirt tenderly on the velvet seat of a Victorian side chair.

As he dressed, Vladimir moved with delicacy and economy. He was nonchalant, unhurried, and almost feline in his grace and poise. His hands were the kind of hands you would notice first.

As they used to say, they were the hands of an artist, a musician—a pianist or a flutist—and they were a pale pastel vermilion and pink as if they had just been soaked in warm, sudsy water. His nails were remarkable. So perfect, in fact, they appeared to have been done in a French manicure, the half moons as if painted with acrylics and a brush by a nail stylist. His lips, a touch more florid than one would think they should be, were swollen into a little bow-tie pucker and carried, at their corners, the softest hint of a perpetual almost imperceptible smile.

As his final act in the ritual of dressing, he placed one of his most prized possessions on his wrist, an aviator's watch, a Breitling Eclipse, a watch capable of tracking the phases of the moon, performing multiplications, divisions, conversions of distances and units, all the while ticking off the seconds of one's life with astonishing, unerring precision. This awesome time machine appeared much too big for Vladimir's slender wrist.

When he had finished dressing, he turned toward the tulips in the vase. Again, he reached out with his long fingers and stroked one of them. He loved flowers. Adored them. Loved to pick them in the garden, loved to arrange them in vases, plant them in pots. On some days he would playfully insert a flower into the third buttonhole of his white shirt. Today, it would be the red bachelor's button that Mrs. Petrovsky had left beside the vase.

He always dressed the same during the day: the white shirt of sheer Egyptian cotton, size fifteen with thirty-five-inch barrel-cuffed pearl-buttoned sleeves, no starch, meticulously ironed by Mrs. Petrovsky; a pair of clerical black tropical wool trousers with front inverted pleats and two-inch cuffs, a thirty-two-inch waist, and thirty-four-inch inseam. His trousers were sharply creased and dropped with a slight break onto the insteps of his double-soled, chestnut burnished calfskin shoes with a strap and buckle at the ankle from Crockett & Jones, Northampton, England. His belt was also tan calfskin, also Crockett & Jones, with an antique gold slip-through buckle engraved with his initials.

While he was busy dressing, Mrs. Petrovsky prepared his breakfast downstairs in the kitchen—the juice of fresh, chilled oranges stirred with a teaspoon of sugar; one-half cup of coffee, a Kona blend brewed from freshly ground Arabica beans; one poached egg carefully placed on a piece of buttered toast on a small porcelain plate, a Limoges with a scalloped, platinum-dipped edge. She sprinkled the egg with sea salt and a dash of freshly ground pepper and then glazed it with a mixture of bacon bits and melted Plugrá butter. Beside that on another porcelain plate she placed a slice of lightly toasted wheat bread. He ate his breakfast alone in the sunroom overlooking the garden.

I'd give all the wealth that years have piled,
The slow result of Life's decay,
To be once more a little child
For one bright summer day.

      — From *Solitude* by Lewis Carroll

Mrs. Petrovsky had founded and ran a ballet school, The Petrovsky School of Classical Ballet, in a Victorian mansion overlooking the river on Glengarry Road in the village of Croton-on-Hudson, New York. The house, built of gray cut stone, had touches of white gingerbread trim, copper rain gutters, gables, leaded and beveled glass windows, a welcoming porch in front, and an English herb and flower garden behind.

She had bought this stately home with new-found wealth acquired through the divorce of a husband, who, by the way, she never spoke of specifically but if asked would freely give her opinion of husbands, if not men in general. "They are most often," she would say, "a dreadful inconvenience, and nearly always an irrelevance."

This opinion did not hinder her from using part of her share of her husband's wealth to surround herself with comfort. So, after buying the big house, she had set about remodeling the interior according to her rather extravagant whims.

She hired the local architect, Reginald Tate, and together they designed two spacious second-floor suites, one for her, the other for Vladimir. Each suite consisted of a living room (they retained the twelve-foot ceilings) with an imposing, formal cut-stone fireplace and a small half-circle mahogany paneled dining nook, a wet bar with a small Sub-Zero refrigerator and icemaker, a little library; a spacious bedroom, a dressing room, a large walk-in closet, and a bath.

Actually the two baths were one, which could be entered from the bedroom of each suite. On Mrs. Petrovsky's side of the bathroom there was not only a giant tub crouching on great ball and claw feet, but a whirlpool Jacuzzi as well as a small sauna.

On Vladimir's side there was a huge marble shower with nozzles at all levels on three sides. Instead of a sauna, he had a small two-person steam room. The sinks on both sides were identical and huge. Their faucets, shaped like two swans with their necks entwined like a caduceus, were gold plated. The floor was pink Venetian tile with a black and green sunburst pattern inlaid in the center.

Each side of the bathroom had its own toilet and bidet. Along the walls were chrome-plated towel warmers like the ones you find in five-star European hotels. And, speaking of European hotels, there were two small Sub-Zero refrigerators set almost invisibly into the wall at the end of the double bathroom. These were stocked with spring water and fresh lemons, and sometimes, on Mrs. Petrovsky's side, with a bottle of Dom Pérignon. On the back of the doors at each end of the dual bathroom was a gold swan's neck hook holding a white terry cloth bathrobe. Of course, one was embroidered "His," the other "Hers."

The parquet floors in the rooms of each suite were scattered, seemingly willy-nilly, in a lavish kaleidoscopic confusion of antique Oriental rugs of various sizes. Vladimir's living room was dominated by a blood red Saruck; hers by an early Chinese Cock rug with fantastic trees and flowers surrounding two majestic multicolored roosters displayed on a rich, *bleu de roi* background. Throughout the suites were Kirman, Abadeh, Bakhtiari,

Kashan, Tekke, Beshir Juval, Ladiks, and at each entry there was an identical Anatolian runner. It was a contemporary decorator's nightmare, a Victorian decorator's dream.

Downstairs, to create one large room, she had removed the wall and French doors between the living room and the formal dining room. She had the parquet floors completely redone: sanded, sealed, varnished, waxed, and then burnished until they had the lustrous patina of wild-flower honey. As this was to be the dance floor, she instructed the workmen to eliminate all the squeaks, "every one," and, so, as she supervised, they tested every inch of the floor and when a squeak was found, they pounced upon it and carefully set finishing nails to silence it. Around the windowless walls, she had floor-to-ceiling mirrors installed. In front of that, the ballerina's barre of polished brass.

The all-white kitchen, like the upstairs double bathroom, was a Clive Christian creation, reflecting Mrs. Petrovsky's obsession with things expensive and continental. It was rather small for such a big home. The white marble countertops, although honed instead of polished, gave it a rather flinty post-modern appearance. The white porcelain sink was double sized, not partitioned and deeper than usual; deep enough, Vladimir once joked, to drown a goose. Even the kitchen floor was white—wide, bleached oak boards. Not surprisingly, the room was filled with light throughout the day, especially in the morning because it faced east, and had a big window, rather a whole series of interlocking mullioned windows overlooking the garden. Its neighboring room, the sunroom, shared the mullioned windows with the kitchen and contributed its own generous donation of natural light.

Emily Spertano and her daughter, Mary, would come to the mansion twice a week, on Tuesdays and Fridays, carrying buckets and mops, a box of Bounty paper towels, bottles of Lysol, and other cleaning paraphernalia. Estelle Walker would come in the early afternoon on weekdays, excepting Thursdays, to prepare the Petrovsky's evening meal. "Both of you," she would laugh, "You eat like little birds. There is no need for tablespoons in this house, only teaspoons and salad plates—oh, those tiny cherry tomatoes, those wee hearts of celery, and the boiled red-skinned potatoes no bigger than marbles."

When they wanted a special meal, something extravagant, something more substantial than the miniature vegetables Mrs. Walker found so remarkable, they would invite Carlos Entarazi, a chef they knew, and he would come up from the city to prepare it for them. The menu would be his choice, and always a surprise, a secret that he would never reveal not even as he prepared the meal or afterwards. He'd let them guess. For example, Carlos once prepared a main course of nuggets of wild boar marinated in buttermilk and seasoned with black pepper, orange, and cinnamon. His repertoire was vast: tiny cheese ravioli with a bright winter-squash sauce, pâtés, wild mushrooms with garlic, braised pork cheeks, rabbit in mustard sauce, fish in crisp brick pastry, and in the wintertime rich game stews black with wine and blood. For dessert there might be rose-scented macaroons filled with rose-petal cream or a small bowl of raspberries or lychee fruit. They never knew what to expect and never cared. Having known the ingredients in some of his entrées, they might never have eaten them. That was the fun of it.

Carlos would have to come on a Monday when his restaurant was closed. He'd come laden with bags and square-handled wicker baskets of groceries and always accompanied by his friend, Carlita, a darkly beautiful, olive-complexioned woman with anthracite hair, emerald eyes, and claret lips.

Carlos and Carlita would complain good-humoredly about the smallness of the kitchen, the scarcity of utensils, but in the end they said it added to the challenge.

These sometime Monday night dinners would be elegant affairs. Mrs. Spertano would polish the silverware array it beside the most delicate bone-white Schumann china and place several sparkling Baccarat crystal glasses at each setting. These would later be filled with the best wines, of course: a Grand Cru Montrachet, pale gold, succulent and sensational; a Curvée Dom Pérignon, of course, ticklishly crisp and chilly; at the penultimate a robust 1975 Fonseca port; and at the very end an assertive Cognac. All with Tchaikovsky playing softly in the background.

Mrs. Petrovsky would dress for these affairs with an extravagance that often rivaled the meal. To add what she called "festivity," she would whisk Carlita upstairs and dress her in some ballerina costume—once even in the risqué almost-nothing she herself had worn in Balanchine's *Seven Deadly Sins.*

"Now, darling, darling, remember," Mrs. Petrovsky would say playfully, "it was Shakespeare who said that 'Brevity is the soul of wit,' but, oh, my darling, it was Dorothy Parker who said, 'Brevity is the soul of lingerie.'"

Carlita would laugh, toss her head, swirl her anthracite hair, pirouette, and then pose flirtatiously before the mirror in Mrs. Petrovsky's bedroom. When she entered, no *danced* into the room downstairs clad in what appeared to be nothing more than a black lace bra and panties; she would cock her head to the side and throw her arms up as if she were Isadora Duncan. Carlos loved it. Vladimir appeared to hardly notice.

On these occasions Vladimir would wear his double-breasted blue blazer and gray flannel pants. He had had the Brooks Brothers hanging lamb insignia buttons replaced with cloisonné buttons depicting the Petrovsky family crest. He would deftly fold a white Irish linen handkerchief into three peaks artfully slanting one shorter than the other like stair steps and place it in the blazer's breast pocket, teasing it down with his long fingers until he had revealed just the right amount of handkerchief. In the lapel he threaded a boutonnière.

For these occasions he would replace his Breitling with an elegant gold Cartier tank watch with a white porcelain face, Roman numerals, and a tan lizard band. He wore no tie and for that Mrs. Petrovsky would admonish him: "Oh, Vladimir, don't you *own* a tie? You look lovely, of course, my dear, but if this were the dinning room at the Waldorf, you'd be turned away at the door. Or made to wear a gravy-stained tie from the headwaiter's closet."

They would eat these lavish sometime Monday meals in the sunroom off the kitchen, which was, in fact, their dining room, the original formal dining room having been sacrificed to create the dance floor area. But the sunroom, so-called, was not small by any means, and the oval Queen Anne table, when set up with all its leaves, could seat twelve. On this table, together, in the late afternoon when a Monday-night dinner was planned, the Petrovskys would inspect the table set by Mrs. Spertano, making sure the white damask tablecloth was properly centered and all the silverware settings, plates, and napkins in their proper place.

When dinner was over, the four of them would pause at the table for a demitasse as black as Carlita's hair and then go into the parlor for a glass of that '75 Fonseca port and a wedge of Stilton.

On these nights nothing was ever cleaned up in the kitchen or taken from the dining table. Pots, pans, glasses, dishes, silverware, dinner plates, all were left where they were. Vladimir would have warned Estelle Walker beforehand so that she could arrange to be there early Tuesday morning to clean up the mess.

Since Mrs. Sperano did not "do dishes," Estelle would wash the china and crystal by hand in the deep porcelain sink, not in the dishwasher, an explicit instruction from Mrs. Petrovsky. The pots and pans could, however, go into the dishwasher. Not the silverware, of course. It would spot.

When a meal was over, with a toss of his hand he would survey the remnants of their dinner and say, "At the end of a feast, alas, behold, no matter how grand, there is nothing left but disarray and garbage. How sad."

After port and Stilton, it would be time for Cognac and that's when Carlos would unveil the Cuban cigars—Cohibas or Montecristos—four of them, the last of his personal contributions to these hedonistic evenings. With great ceremony, he would snip them one by one with his gold-plated "v" guillotine cutter, pierce them with his little silver Tiffany cigar piercer, and pass them around the table. Then he would go round the table, starting with Mrs. Petrovsky, and light them one by one with a propane-powered brûlée torch from the kitchen.

The ladies never finished their cigars—knowing this Carlos actually gave them Honduran or Nicaraguan cigars onto which he had slipped Cohiba or Montecristo rings proclaiming *hecho a mano en Cuba.* Vladimir was in on the fraud and while the men finished their cigars and listened to music, Mrs. Petrovsky would accompany Carlita upstairs to change into her street clothes. When they returned, Vladimir would call a taxi. They would say their "good nights," and when the taxi arrived, Carlos would pick up the white envelope with his name on it from the top of the table in the vestibule, pick up the empty wicker baskets, and, with a sleepy Carlita at his side, depart for the last train to Manhattan.

After they left, the Petrovskys would stand in the vestibule, gently kiss each other on the cheek, congratulate themselves on an evening well spent, turn out the lights, and go upstairs to bed, pausing for cheek-kissing again in the hallway before parting to enter their individual suites.

Lay your sleeping head, my love,
Human on my faithless arm:
Time and fevers burn away
Individual beauty from
Thoughtful children, and the grave
Proves the child ephemeral.
　　— From "Lay your sleeping head, my love"
　　　　　　　　　by W. H. Auden

After breakfast, Vladimir would wander for a while in the garden, inspecting the flowers and herbs, smoking a Tareyton filter tip cigarette, which he held in the European manner between index finger and thumb. Later, when the girls arrived with their dance bags, he would stand in the hallway, smile and greet them with a slight benign and courtly bow, calling their names each in turn, and saying "Good morning," with a studied extravagance to their mothers.

All the mothers loved him for his elegance, polish, and continental manners. Some may even have had warmer, more flirtatious thoughts. He titillated some. Others thought him queer.

"Oh, you know, Jane, he's so … so … well, 'continental,'" said Elaine.

"You mean 'cosmopolitan.'"

"I mean whatever I mean, and you know what I mean."

"Go ahead and say what you really think," said Lori. "He's got a nice rear end."

"I never said that. And, if I had, would that make me a bad person?" Elaine giggled. "Or should I just say he's in such *good* shape? I like the way he moves."

"Oh, my God, Elaine!"

"Come on, girls," said Jane, "what's more important ... well, what's *most* important, is that all the girls just adore him. He's so *good* with them."

"I wonder if he'd be *good* with me, " said Elaine.

"Don't you wonder," said Lori, "if he's not a little, well, odd?"

"Do you mean gay? said Elaine. "

"Will you for heaven sakes stop?" said Jane. "You're both incorrigible. Elaine, do you know what? You and Lori need a vacation. You need to go somewhere to get this smuttiness out of your system."

"That's not what I need," said Elaine.

"Could we lift this conversation to a higher level?" said Jane.

"I'll stop. I was only kidding."

"Well," said Jane, "all that aside, I do know that we *are* lucky to have the Petrovsky's here. They're such a positive influence on our girls. Really. Such positive role models. Ballet, classical music, exercise, elegance, what more could we ask for?"

"In other words, girls, what the hell would we do without them? said Lori."

And so the mothers of Croton-on-Hudson and the nearby river towns brought their little darlings, young girls between the ages of six and twelve—the supple years, Mrs. Petrovsky called them—to the school on Glengarry Road. At any given time, there would be only ten of them, for in spite of the school's being popular and well established, Mrs. Petrovsky strictly limited the enrollment to that number. Period. Thus, a new student could come under the tutelage of Mrs. Petrovsky only when another left. Or graduated. There was a waiting list, but, truth be told, it was never honored if a more talented prospect came along.

Mrs. Petrovsky's mother, a widow, emigrated from Russia to America, bringing her only child with her. Mother and daughter settled in the Kensington section of Brooklyn where the mother immediately set about the task of grooming her daughter to become a ballerina.

The child first touched the barre at the age of six, at a small, somewhat gritty Russian ballet school. By the age of eighteen she was one of George Balanchine's favorite little ballerinas. Now, after traveling the world with Balanchine, she was a woman of a certain age, who had retained her own balletic suppleness with a regimen adopted from *Allegra Kent's Water Beauty Book.*

She pursued her water exercises whenever she took a mind to in the sapphire waters of the indoor pool at the Fletcher's. She supplemented her water workouts with two hours of Pilates usually two times a week. Mrs. Fletcher joined her for these callisthenic classes, which were conducted by a man named Emilio Laternes, who came up on the train from Manhattan. And, of course, she kept her figure taut by eating, as Emily Spertano noted, the diet of a sparrow, or perhaps one should say the diet of a rabbit.

Mrs. Petrovsky's eyes were an intense, almost neon blue. So very blue, in fact, that several of the students' mothers thought she wore tinted contact lenses. Her hair was a splendid mixture of silvery white and gold, a sheer platinum color. She did it up herself into a tight French twist that looked as if it had been carved from bleached ash wood meticulously oiled and pumiced to a soft, satin sheen. Her thighs, as seemingly polished and as luminous as her hair, were firm and perfectly tapered. Her arms were the same. Her stomach, flat as a platter, sloped down and disappeared into the triangle between her legs. Her skin, a delicate dusty, peachy rose was always a perfect complement to her black leotards. Her speech, lightly accented with Russian, was incredibly melodic as if it were meant only to recite poetry. When she spoke to her students, her every word was nothing but a poetic melody of tutelage, compliment, and encouragement.

While Mrs. Petrovsky instructed the students, it was Vladimir's job to assist with the everyday details of running the school: ushering the girls to the changing room, arranging and selecting the costumes, selecting the music, supervising and scheduling the pianist, recording the sessions in a ledger for each child, and so on. The school was their world. Their only world. She was the ethereal ballerina, he the ever attentive dance master.

And Mrs. Petrovsky was ever attentive to her darling dance master. In fact, rather lavish in her attentions. Three years ago, for his birthday, she bought him a cobalt blue Jaguar 3.8 liter S-type sedan, which like the Brits, she called their "Jag-ū-ar." It had a biscuit leather interior, which is just a bit lighter than *café au lait,* with chestnut-brown piping; a Goldie custom sunroof that opened with the touch of a finger and closed with the flick of a wrist; red-line Michelin tires mounted on chrome wire wheels; a walnut veneer dashboard framing the Lucas gauges and walnut veneer trays that popped out with a touch from behind each of the front seats.

On either side of the rear seats were matching vanity sets also veneered in walnut. The one on the left contained a small red enamel clothes brush, a vesta or match case, a sterling silver cigarette case, and a tiny ashtray. The one on the right contained a small hand mirror, two glass-faced powder jars, a perfume bottle, and a small leather notepad, all accented with red enamel fittings. The door to the one on the left bore a silver inset St. Christopher medallion. The one on the right, a small Waltham timepiece, also inset.

Emily Spertano's son Tony kept Vladimir's Jaguar as clean and polished as a hearse. He bought a new, extra stiff toothbrush once a month at Carnaby's Drugs and dipped it in a mild detergent to scrub the wire wheels and brighten the red line in the tires. Once a month he also carefully wound the little Waltham clock.

Given the size of Croton and the nature of their lives, the car was not often used. On Thursdays, if she decided to go there, Mrs. Petrovsky might drive it over to the Fletcher's pool. But if she went shopping, she'd go down to the city on the train. Vladimir used it only to drive to Croton Point Park every now and then for picnics with the girls, or he might drive over to the Croton Dam or occasionally to Croton Point in the evening to view a sunset on the river. Sometimes he'd drive to the ruins at Finney Farm, which they used on occasion as a set for dance recitals.

Many of these trips, most in fact, were not more than a few miles, many less than two. Sometimes, but of course not always, he would drive down to the station to pick up Carlos and Carlita when they came up from the city to cook those occasional lavish Monday dinners; and on Tuesdays, he might drive down to pick up Emilio. But there were taxis at the station so neither of these trips were regular occurrences. Therefore, the Jaguar stayed like new.

How can we know the dancer from the dance?
— From *Among School Children* by W.B. Yeats

Constance Carmichael, age eleven, entered the Petrovsky's comfortable world late one afternoon in April, as if she were a flower flushed from the damp earth by the chilly rains of that cruelest month. She stood in the hallway beside her mother, a little blush-cheeked child no taller than the balustrade. In her bright yellow slicker, and matching goulashes, she looked like a giant daffodil

It was Vladimir who thought she looked like a giant daffodil enfolded with what he loved the most in these little girls, what he called "petals of innocence." As he looked at her, he felt that some soft aura surrounded her. He felt that he was standing within the encirclement of some kind of sweetly celestial luminosity. A halo. And in the air he sensed an unknown fragrance, a perfume he had never smelled before.

"Good afternoon, Mrs. Carmichael," he said without taking his eyes off Constance. "And you must be little Constance. Mrs. Petrovsky will be down in a moment. Here, Mrs. Carmichael, Constance. Let me take your coats. You can sit here." He motioned to the settee in the foyer as he threw the coats over the balustrade.

"Well, Constance, what do you think? There's not very much to see around here, the barre, the mirrors, the polished floors, and the piano. Well, there are all these pictures, Mrs. Petrovsky's pictures, pictures of her past glory, her years with the New York City Ballet, with Balanchine and all that." With a theatrical gesture, he raised his arm toward a Fred Fehl photograph of his mother in black lace underwear leaping on stage; her head thrown back, arms outstretched performing in Balanchine's *Seven Deadly Sins.* Then he pointed to another, a photograph of a *pas de deux* showing Mrs. Petrovsky draped seductively over Arthur Mitchell's arm in the ballet *Agon.*

Little Constance stood at his side staring raptly at the pictures. He held her hand.

One cannot look at such pictures—indeed, perhaps one could say at any pictures—of the dance and dancers (if not especially ballet) without thinking about the essential sexuality and sensuality of dance. A critic commenting on an exhibition of Degas's work once said, "Edgar Degas loved dancers but loathed women." He noted that the artist's sketchbooks were filled with ". . . ballerinas in their feline lassitude, warming their muscles before class or engaged in other rituals of the body." One thinks immediately of Degas's well-known sculpture, *The Little Fourteen-Year-Old Dancer.*

Dance so often celebrates the rituals of the body and the emotions that surround seduction and lovemaking. Perhaps no dance is a better exemplar of this than the "Dance of the Seven Veils" made famous by Colette's 1907 performance at the Moulin Rouge. And, whether he went there for stimulation or inspiration, it is said that George Balanchine, before he came to America, would spend many of his evenings at one of Paris's saloons, the Crazy Horse—they were actually, in modern parlance, strip clubs. Classical ballet, therefore, might be considered simply a higher form of this celebration of the seductive and the sensual. But the ballet dancer is not a stripper. She comes on the stage already stripped. In his *Seven Deadly Sins,* Balanchine has dispensed with the seven veils in favor of black lace underwear.

Thus Constance and Vladimir stood there before the thirty or more

photographs of Mrs. Petrovsky, a collection that might easily be perceived
by the prurient eye as worthy, indeed, of posters for the strip clubs of
Paris. And as if to legitimize as art this gallery of pictures, which might
otherwise seem risqué, were dozens of framed reviews of Mrs. Petrovsky's
performances clipped from the *New York Times*.

At the end of the hall, Vladimir, still holding Constance's hand, said,
"Oh, yes, of course, there are dressing and changing rooms. Closets. A
bathroom. And a place for the girls to leave their dance bags."

He walked back up the hall with Constance and seated her beside her
mother on the settee.

"Darling, this is Vladimir Petrovsky," said Mrs. Carmichael., touching
Constance lightly on the shoulder.

"Oh, please, pardon me for not introducing myself," apologized
Vladimir.

"He is the Dance Master, Mrs. Petrovsky's son."

"Delighted to meet you, Mr. Petrovsky. 'Dance Master,' how very
powerful that sounds." Her voice had that perfect modulation and
sophistication that the voices of children raised among adults always seem to
have. How well schooled her politeness, how perfectly relaxed she was, how
natural and warm her smile. How innocent the redness of her little lips.

"Oh, no, Constance I have very little power here. Really. And, besides,
you are not here to meet me. You are here to meet Mrs. Petrovsky, the great
ballerina. She's the one with the 'power' around here."

As if his statement were timed as her introduction, Mrs. Petrovsky
entered the room. "Entered," of course, is the wrong word. She did
something more than that. It was as if the dimmer on the lights had been
turned up, as if the sun had come out from behind the clouds and pierced
the window with a shaft of light.

She was dressed in black tights with a lemony chiffon wrap cascading
from her shoulders to the floor. It swirled around her like incense smoke.
With only a hint of makeup, she was flawless. With her sparkling electric
blue eyes, the velvety pink pouting lips, the natural, subtle rouge of her
cheeks, she was the very portrait and definition of a ballerina. In her
presence, any dampness from the rain droplets on the Carmichaels'

raincoats seemed to vaporize. Any aura that Constance herself may have momentarily lent to the room was swept away. Gone. The room was now filled with and belonged exclusively to Mrs. Petrovsky, the prima ballerina.

"So, my dear, you are Constance Carmichael." Mrs. Petrovsky ignored the mother and bent down toward the little girl, hands outstretched. "Vladimir, you did not hang their coats up! How thoughtless of you!" And, turning to Constance she said, "Here, my dear, let me look at you."

Constance rose from the settee. She wore a little unbuttoned vest over her blouse and Mrs. Petrovsky's hands flew like birds under the shoulders of the vest, peeled it back in one motion sending it to the floor like a discarded banana peel.

"Turn around, my dear. That's right. Gorgeous! You are gorgeous. Ah, but can you dance? Vladimir, show Constance to the changing room. I'll talk to her mother and then we'll dance together, Constance, you and I. We'll dance. Take her, Vladimir, take her."

He reached out and touched Constance on her shoulder, steering her down the hallway to the dressing room. Constance marveled at the length of his fingers and the size of his watch.

Soon afterward, Constance was accepted into the school. But on that first day, in the foyer, fresh from the April rain, she had entered the consciousness of Vladimir in a most curious and mysterious way.

Wee, modest, crimson-tipped flow'r,
Thou's met me in an evil hour;
For I maun crush amang the stoure
Thy slender stem:
To spare thee now is past my pow'r, Thou bonie gem.
— From *To a Mountain Daisy* by Robert Burns

How does a thought possess one's mind and sweep away other thoughts? What does this word "possess" mean? How do we possess things or people? How, for example, does a hunter possess his prey? Why, through stalking and killing, of course. The hunter possesses the animal he preys upon through its death. Is death then an instrument of possession? If so, why do we call death a loss when, as in the hunter's case, it appears to be a gain? Do we not *grieve* for "the loss" of a loved one? Yet we say it is the world's loss, heaven's gain. Does the hunter grieve for the loss of his prey? Or does he rejoice in the possession of his prey? Does he not love his prey and pursue it passionately? Surely he does not hate it. No, clearly, he loves his prey. Finds excitement and enjoyment in its pursuit. Witness that when he comes upon the animal lying dead by his hand, he kneels and strokes its head, fondles its horns, pats its shoulder, smoothes its fur, and kneels beside it to admire its beauty. He is elated by the emotion engendered by now at last possessing it. There is no grieving. No moral reckoning. Only rejoicing.

Isn't it all a game? This whole possession thing? Some mysterious game of hide and seek, stalk and find. Is not seduction a sport that leaves one wondering who is the possessor and who the possessed?

With Vladimir, these thoughts swarmed around the singular thought of Constance, this bright and pretty child. But that single thought had exploded and became a million thoughts, a searing sleet of thoughts. A thunderstorm of thoughts. He began to wonder if Constance had become an obsession—some dark obsession released by the thought of Constance?

He began slowly to realize that he wanted not so much to possess Constance as to possess what she was, the idea of her: innocence, youth, purity, beauty. But her sophistication made it difficult to think of her as a mere child. And that's what he wanted to do, to bask in the illumination of her youth and innocence. That's what attracted him to her in the first place and now transformed him into, well, a bee that visits flowers and extracts a portion of their scent and sweetness.

He was a bee. Constance was a flower. He could feed on the pollen of her innocence without destroying it. Wasn't that possible? That's how he felt. He could simply extract the nectar from Constance. That would be enough. It would be enough to extract her nectar but would that not be her innocence? Remove the innocence and the obsession would be gone. Was that true? What if that were true? If not he, then someone else at some other time in some other place. Or time itself would do the deed. In time, maturity would steal all her April-ness anyway. Her innocence would, even if he were not the thief, disappear one day like flowers disappear, like flowers bloom, unfold, flourish, wither, and die. That would happen, of course. But if not like a bee taking pollen from a flower would he be like the season's first frost descending in the night upon the last flowers of summer, extracting their color, vigor, and, finally, their very life itself?

These thoughts tormented him. Was extracting innocence from April's children like nothing more than extracting pollen from flowers. Bees destroy nothing. Bees do not harm the flowers they visit. Bees help flowers grow and flourish and enjoy their time in the sun. The hives are awake in the spring and the hunt for nectar begins. And "the honey of April is the most limpid and perfumed of all."

Mrs. Petrovsky brought flowers to her bee everyday. He never had to go in search of them. They were always there for him. There was always a bouquet of flowers for him to choose from.

O stonyhearted race, more savage than any wild beast, to find cruel amusement in bitter murder!
— From *Epigrammata,19* by Thomas More

T he living room of Vladimir's upstairs suite was a virtual child's playhouse. It was cluttered like an untidy toyshop, filled with toppling stacks of games and innumerable dolls of every description and toys beyond naming. Music boxes with twirling ballerinas, clowns, and dancing bears. A circular rack holding a rainbow of costumes. Little chairs with satin and brocade seats, tiny rockers, and a big couch. Strewn about were fanciful pillows of all kinds, sizes and shapes. Sitting in front of the fireplace were stuffed bears, tigers, and dinosaurs—big and little—, from F.A.O. Schwartz.

There was a complete Bang & Oulfsen audio system, a machine almost as ingenious as his watch, complete with a rosewood and brushed aluminum receiver, a tape player that sprang to life with a touch. It could scroll through a tape and find songs and play them once or many times, and there was a Beogram 3404 turntable. To feed this wondrous music machine, there were stacks upon stacks of tapes and records in their colorful cardboard sleeves scattered everywhere.

The windows were hung with velvet drapes the color of Amarone wine. They were controlled with a wall switch, which launched tiny electric trolleys to pull them open or closed. The whole room, it seemed, could be controlled with the touch of a finger. Touch one button and music plays. Touch another and the drapes open or close. Touch another and the lights dim or brighten.

Vladimir took great delight in his playroom. During breaks and rest periods he would bring the girls up there, two and three at a time. The girls would roll and tussle on the huge couch, toss pillows at each other, marvel at the music boxes and the Bang & Olufsen with its ability to pick songs and play them at the touch of a button.

"Come upstairs," he would say, holding out his hand. "I have something wonderful to show you. Come upstairs and we'll play." It was his job to entertain the children, to keep them happy, to make their time at the school not all work and no play.

His little friends loved the vast bathroom, too. Vladimir let them play there, games of hide and seek, but he never let them run the water for fear it would ruin their dresses. And he never let them open the door to the bedroom of his mother's suite.

There would be tea parties for his little "sisters" in the garden, too. Estelle would make dainty cucumber sandwiches with the crust trimmed off and there would be ladyfingers and sometimes chocolate chip cookies, macaroons, and brownies, and they would bring them into the garden on silver trays. They would sing and dance and tell stories or just sit there and listen to the birdsongs and the buzz of bees.

The little girls—and their mothers, too—were delighted with Vladimir's attentions. The mothers loved the idea of the playroom—what trouble and expense he had gone to!—and the fact that Vladimir would take time to entertain the girls between their sessions downstairs. They would say, "He is so wonderful with the children; why they adore him." The girls, would cling to Vladimir and hang on his every word. He would sing them songs, tell them stories, recite poems—some made up on the spot. They would bounce on the big sofa and rock in the little rocking chairs while they listened.

The only room in his suite that was off limits was his bedroom. And the attic above it.

"No one can know how I have loved ... the ways of the things of slender limbs, of fine nose, of great eager ears, of mild wary eyes, and of vague and half-revealed forms and colors. ... I have so loved them that I longed to kill them."

— William Thompson quoted in
Hunting with The Bow and Arrow by S. Pope

V ladimir and Constance were sitting together on the couch, only the two of them in the toy-strewn room. He looked at her and said, "Constance, do you love me?"

She was on his lap dressed in black leotards facing him. "Don't be silly; of course I do. I always will."

"Will you kiss me then?"

"Yes, here's your kiss." She leaned forward and kissed him lightly on the lips.

"Oh, what a sweet kiss! May I have another?"

"One's enough. That's your ration for the day."

"Well, then I'll have to steal one."

"Oh, no, you won't." She hopped down from his lap.

"Vladimir, come on. Let's just play."

"But we *are* playing, Constance."

"If this is playing, I don't like the game anymore."

"Of course you do. You know you do.

"Please. Let's stop."

"But this is a game. Let's make it a love-story game. You are the princess. I am the prince, no, wait, I am the *king*. The all-powerful king."

"Vladimir, I want to play some music."

"What? You're not listening to me. Are you scared? What could you be scared of? The evil king?"

"I'm not scared."

"You're scared of me?"

"Of course I'm not."

"Do you want to run away from me?"

"No. I just want to play another game, really to play some music."

"OK, let's go back and pretend that I am the evil king and you are my prisoner. No wonder you're scared." Vladimir reached out and stroked her hair. "Now isn't that better?"

"Much."

"Are you afraid of the evil king? Afraid that he will lock you in a dungeon and everyday steal all the kisses he wants?"

"Well, that doesn't scare me. Just gives me, well, a feeling. I don't know what it is."

"It is not fear is it?"

"Mmmm. No, it's not really fear, I suppose. But I guess if I *were* the prisoner of an evil king, I would, I should be *very* scared."

"Well, what if you were my prisoner, how scared would you be then? Ah, I know. How scared would you be if you were a prisoner of, not the evil king, but, instead, a prisoner of love?"

"Vladimir, you're being silly. This is a really stupid game. And you *are* being very, very silly."

"Well, we are just playing evil king and captured princess. You are a prisoner of love and if you escape, that will end the game.

"Then, sir, end the game I shall. There I've escaped. I'm free!"

It was not exactly the game that had made her afraid. What it had done, however, is awaken in her some unknown, as yet unrecognized emotion. She did not feel the cold finger of fear so much as a warmly serene detachment as if she were in a slow unstoppable pirouette. No, she was not afraid. Not really. She had no idea what it would mean to be "a prisoner of love."

She sauntered, indeed, like a princess across the room to select a record from the pile.

"Let there be music! Now that I am no longer *a prisoner of love*, I want to hear music. Oh, evil king, may I put a record on the turntable. Music, they say it has the power to sooth the heart of the savage beast."

"Of course you can."

He leaned back and closed his eyes. In a moment, he was launched into a dream, and in the dream he was standing on the summit of a mountain as high as the Matterhorn. A violent storm roared through the valley below. The thunder, in a voice like that of Zeus, said, "I will touch you and you will burst into flames."

Vladimir knew that he had nearly embarked on a dangerous journey— but it was a journey he had never consciously meant to take. It was a momentary, subliminal compulsion, and when it happened, it was like an out-of-body experience—this was not he; he was not that person on the couch. He was a celestial observer floating above the couch, looking down on a child and a man.

When he awoke from his dream, Constance was rocking in one of the small rockers listening to the music. He wanted to say to her, "Forgive me, Constance. Forgive me. I never meant to scare you." He thought: *Have I discovered a beast in my own heart? Dear God, deliver me from the beast in my heart.*

8

To most people incest is even more unthinkable than murder.
— From *Ungentlemanly Acts* by Louise Barnett

Mrs. Petrovsky came into his room that morning with the vase of fresh flowers. It was an unusually colorful and fragrant spring bouquet. She had just bathed and her skin was still warm and flushed. Its fragrance rivaled the fragrance of the flowers. Her cascade of unbound hair, perfumed and just barely damp, curled up as it touched her shoulders like the riffles in a woodland stream.

"How sweet you look in sleep, my love. How many secrets do you bear in that sweet head?" She bent over to kiss him, first on his cheek, then lightly on his lips. Her tongue could not resist. It flicked one tender time deftly parting the bow of his sleeping lips and then darting between them.

She wore a satin lace-topped teddy of the faintest, palest mint green, and when she bent over this second time her breasts hovered inquiringly over Vladimir's face. She knelt over him and rolled her right shoulder downward until the spaghetti strap slid down her arm completely revealing her right breast. She leaned over and sank closer to him allowing her bare breast to descend behind the curtain of her platinum hair until it nestled lightly on his lips. At the touch, Vladimir's lips parted reflexively.

In his dream, he was in the garden and had impulsively plucked the bud from a tulip tree. He held the bud gently between his lips, and, mistaking the warmth of his lips for the warmth of the sun, the bud was now stirring, swelling.

She closed her eyes and arched the small of her back, still holding her breast to his lips.

"There, there, my darling," she said in the softest possible whisper, again closing her eyes, tilting her head back, arching her back, "Oh, my darling boy."

She pressed her breast to his lips, more firmly, more flagrantly now. In his dream he opened his mouth. She kept her breast pressed against his mouth, rhythmically rolling her shoulder until her body tensed and trembled as a wave of warmth washed over her. A moment after it passed, she tensed and trembled again.

She raised her head and opened her eyes. She rolled back on her kneeling legs and brought her torso upright. She relaxed and pulled the spaghetti strap back onto her shoulder. She knelt there for a moment beside his bed, then she brushed her hair back, smiled, and leaned forward until her lips hovered a millimeter above his. She breathed sweet, moist breath between his parted lips and into his mouth. Then she kissed those lips with a mother's tenderness and whispered, "Oh, Vladimir, my lovely, lovely darling boy. We shall always be together."

His eyes were tightly closed. In his dream he was walking in the garden; he could feel the breeze on his lips.

Some men ... seem to enjoy feeling evil; and some hunters ...
may enjoy their sport precisely because it makes them feel wild
and wicked and crazy.
— From *A View to a Death in The Morning*
by Matt Cartmill

It was not wrong; she knew that in her heart. She knew that loving a son was not wrong; it cannot possibly be wrong to love your only child, to love any child of yours, as it cannot be wrong to love yourself. A child, a son, after all, is part of a mother's body and is it not in all the world, among all species, a mother's duty to see to the pleasure and happiness of her child, to educate her child in the ways of the world, to protect her child from any evil in the world, to make a nest for her child well out of harm's reach, to share her warmth, her breath, her love with her child?

Man, proud man ... is able to ... take pleasure in the pain he deliberately ... sets out to cause. It is clearly absurd to speak of his conduct as 'brutal.' Rather we should call it devilish, the Devil usually being credited with a goodly share of intelligence.

— From *The Biological Aspects of Warfare,*
by Harry Campbell

Vladimir awoke with no memory of his dream to find the vase of fresh flowers. He sat up and smiled at his mother's thoughtfulness. He touched each flower one by one with his fingers as if they were piano keys. Then, he stroked them with the palm of his hand as if he were smoothing a young girl's hair. Then he bent down to kiss them one by one, then plunged his face into them playfully. He moved it through them, left, right, up, down, again as if they were a girl's hair. Then he looked up, startled by his own actions.

How bestial, he thought, to root around like a pig in a bouquet of flowers. He took one of them and stuffed it into his mouth, clenched it between his teeth and pressed it with his tongue. Suddenly, a bright fragment of last night's dream flashed in his brain—the tulip-tree bud;

it was in his mouth. Immediately, he spit it out. What's the matter with me," he thought?

"Why can I not remember dreams? Why do they so quickly descend into our subconscious? Why are dreams so elusive, so ephemeral? Why can I not remember them at will? Could it be that we do not want to remember dreams? That we are not meant to remember *some* dreams?"

He licked his lips. He could still taste the flower bud. Impulsively, he grabbed another one, crushed it in his fist to release its fragrant juices; then brought his fist to his nose and inhaled deeply. He thought, Oh, yes, yes, now I seem to recall what in my dream was more like the delicate fragrance and sweet taste of , of just-washed flesh. Yes, but I recall I was in the garden …."

Enjoyed no sooner but despised straight
Past reason hunted, and no sooner had
Past reason hated as a swallow's bait
On purpose laid to make the taker mad.
— From Sonnet CXXIX,
by William Shakespeare

On warm summer days, Vladimir would ask the mothers of his favorites for permission to take them for a picnic to Croton Point Park down by the Hudson River. Who would not want to pile into Vladimir's elegant Jaguar and go for a picnic by the river in the park?

The children Vladimir selected for these outings would run out to the car, peeling down their front walks like little bells in chiffon and cotton sundresses. We are going for a ride! We're going to have a picnic! But once in the car they would behave like ladies,. They would open the pop-down trays and the vanities and demurely pretend to powder their noses. They would take turns placing their ears against the Waltham to see if it was ticking. And off to the river they would go. Vladimir would look up from time to time into the rearview mirror to see those little bundles of cotton and chiffon tumbling around in the back seat of the Jaguar—one of the girls would have the place of honor riding up front with the Dance Master himself.

Vladimir had a circa 1920s wicker picnic hamper. On back of the hinged lid were leather straps holding down an assortment of picnic knives, forks, and spoons. The inside of the hamper was fitted with compartments holding plates and glasses along with black and red enamel containers, and two bottles with woven wicker covers.

The girls thought the hamper "very cool," and when it was removed from the trunk of the car, they would gather around for its opening. And the opening ceremony went like this: Vladimir would set it on the picnic table, right in the center, and square it up with much scrutinizing to determine its precise location on the table. Then he would hold his hands, palms down, over it as if he were a priest at mass holding his hands over a chalice. His eyes would be closed. With head tilted back, he would say, forcing his voice into a low baritone, "Open, oh, great hamper, venerable visitor from another time. Open, oh, great cornucopia of plenty. Open and reveal the secrets of the succulent feast hidden within thy depths—with dear Estelle's help!" As he spoke these words, the girls would dance around the table like Indians, singing solemn-sounding nonsense songs. "Wigga wa wigga wa wigga wa woo."

As she did for their garden tea parties, Estelle would, indeed, work magic. She would fill, no, literally stuff the hamper with dainty cucumber sandwiches, some cut with a cookie cutter into heart shapes, others into diamonds. She would fill one of the black enamel containers with mixed salad and tiny cherry tomatoes seasoned with salt, pepper and sprinkled with Caluccio extra-virgin olive oil and a dash of Balsamic vinegar. For dessert, she would fill another of the black enamel containers with ladyfingers or a stack of lemon squares, and sometimes there would even be a small package of chocolate chip cookies or the tiniest of brownies. Of course, the wicker bottles would be filled with enough cold, tart lemonade to slack the thirst of all of the guests. And there would be a thermos of hot tea.

Once seated at the picnic table, the guests, each with their lunch selected from among the hamper's treasures and arrayed on platters before them, would begin to mock-beg Vladimir—"Please, oh, please, oh, please, please, oh, please, a story, a *new* story, kind sir. Please, oh great Dance Master, tell us a *new* story."

Vladimir would launch into a story with no hesitation. "Once upon a time there lived an evil fox and a good rabbit. …" After the story was told and the sandwiches, salad, cookies, and lemonade consumed, he would pour hot tea from the thermos into porcelain demitasse cups, add a dash of milk, and allow the little ladies to spoon in all the sugar they desired. Then it was time for a song.

After that one or two of the girls would walk down to the breakwater by the riverside. Vladimir would light a cigarette—much to their disapproval but it was nonetheless an excitingly evil thing for him to do, and they relished that. He and the girls still remaining around the picnic table would lie on their backs on a plaid stadium blanket spread near the table on the grass. For this purpose, Vladimir always fetched a small pillow from the car. After he spread the blanket and tossed the pillow on it, he would set the alarm on the Waltham and leave the back door of the car open so they could hear it go off because all the mothers had expectations as to exactly when their daughters would return. Vladimir would not want to disappoint them.

Croton Point Park was a lovely place. A place where cedar picnic tables reposed in the cool shade under the limbs of giant mature oak trees. A place where the lawn spread like a vast emerald tablecloth right up to the water's edge where it was stopped by a cement-topped stone breakwater that you could walk upon. At this point the majestic Hudson flowed nearly two hundred yards wide from shore to shore, and in the spring and summer its entire width was dotted with the sails of dozens and dozens of meandering boats big and small. In the winter, if it was an especially cold winter, say in February, there would be iceboats with sails of fluorescent orange and electric green skipping and skittering at breakneck speed across the river's washboard surface. In fact, during really, really cold winters, the Hudson at Croton Point would freeze almost entirely presenting a chilly Shakeltonian vision of ice and snow.

But there was one small problem with the park. To enjoy its pastoral beauty, you first had to drive down the dusty, potholed macadam road that formed the northern boundary of the Croton Dump, a vast and ghastly landfill inhabited by rats the size of rabbits. (Boys would shoot them for sport with BB guns and ball bearings hurled with deadly speed and accuracy from wrist rockets.) There were wild dogs, feral cats, and always overhead were squadrons of gliding, diving, screeching gulls. In fact, the standard answer to the question "How do you get to Croton-on-Hudson?" was "Follow the gulls."

Giant yellow front loaders and bulldozers worked ceaselessly, chugging to and fro across the surface of the dump, emitting diesel grunts and groans and squeaks as they arranged and rearranged the mountains of refuse brought everyday by an endless stream of belching, rumbling trucks. Hovering above the dump, like a pot lid, was a pale mustard-colored, stingingly acrid, foul-smelling haze of dust and putrid smoke.

The incredible ugliness of the dump and its raucous hustle-bustle was a jarring contrast to the serenity of the park itself. It acted like the park's burly bodyguard and gatekeeper, for no matter how enticing was the pastoral ambience of the park, one had to enter it through this Dantean landscape just as one must pass through a smoldering purgatory to enter heaven. Many Crotonites, therefore, even if they could have had Dante's Beatrice by their side, chose not to pass through this purgatory to enter the park. Vladimir Petrovsky was, of course, not among those timid souls. As a consequence he and his dainty dancers often had the park all to themselves save for the few fishermen who were always sitting on the edge of the breakwater.

Thus, on sunny days in late spring and early summer, if one peeked through the smoke of the smoldering dump, one might see Vladimir and his playmates picnicking in the park. Why, even in the winter, on milder days, he would take the braver ones down there. They'd all be bundled up and wrapped tight in multi-colored scarves that fell to their knees. They would stand hand-in-hand muscling precariously into the wind, standing on the breakwater until their cheeks grew apple red and the dampness froze into frost on their mittens.

Their passage through this purgatorial smog served to make the journey to the park all the more exciting. In the summer, for example, when the stench along the broken macadam approach road was ripest, Vladimir would open the Jaguar's sunroof, slow down, stick his hand out the top and playfully cupping it, encourage the fumes to enter the car. Then he would blow air through his lips, making a *brrr-brr-prr-prr* sound, whinnying like a horse, making a fearsome grimace and reaching down to pinch his nostrils shut. In their turn the girls would do the same, *brrr-brr-prr-prr-ing* and giggle uncontrollably.

Then, when the din and dust and stench parted to reveal the glory of the park, he would accelerate the car, the girls' heads would jerk back and he would always say, "No fretting now, my ladies. How can we enjoy the bright, sunny days of our lives if we have not known storm, adversity, smog, and darkness?"

So, for all of them it was fun to go down the bumpy, dusty road and to break out of that disagreeable region into the heavenly brilliance of the park—more fun, certainly, than had the park been accessible through some pristine, tree-lined boulevard.

They made quite a picture there in the park on those sunny summer afternoons: this tall, thin Pied Piper strolling down to the water's edge with a gaggle of girls in jonquil dresses. So pretty a sight that it would never fail to bring a warm smile to the face of even the most hardened observer. The girls, like animated flowers, would dance in the river's breezes. He would look like a character out of Gosford Park—dressed as he was on these occasions in white flannel pants, his customary long-sleeved white shirt, and his elegant ankle boots with strap and buckle.

His summer park-and-picnic costume was crowned with a splendid, creamy, black-banded Panama hat, worn because, as Vladimir was quick to warn, "Beware, beware the summer sun, my dears; it is the enemy of our youth and beauty."

Our lives are often the result of who we are told we are—not who we are.

— From *Always a Woman* by Kaylan Pickford

One day, having gone to the park alone, Vladimir stared out across the wide Hudson River. His thoughts were of his father.

"I wonder where my father is?" he thought. "Without my father, without a father, how can I know how to be a man? I wonder, does he, wherever he is, does he ever think of me? I wonder what *would* he think of me? Does he ever wonder how I've turned out? Would he love me, understand me, or would he hate me? Or think me queer? Maybe not. Look, father I have a big, aviator's chronometer, a Breitling, a rich man's watch. I live well, and I know that I have you to thank for that. If you were here, what would we be doing now? Standing here looking at the Hudson? Or, perhaps, fly fishing for brown trout in the Croton River, or sailing on the Hudson? Or hiking in the hills? But you are *not* here. Instead I am here, and I am alone, save for my little child friends. I am here alone as if floating in a bowl of flowers, a meaningless world of child's play. Oh, of course, I have my mother. Do you ever think of my mother?"

Vladimir raised his head to trace the flight of a gull soaring purposefully up the river. He thought of a line of dialogue from some film he had once seen and never forgotten. In the film, two horsemen—dusty, trail-weary cowboys—stop to look up at a hawk soaring high above them. "Look at that," says one of the cowboys, "she'll be flying over the Musselshell in, oh, what do you think? I'd say, oh, maybe an hour, maybe two. Take us up to four days hard riding." The other cowboy said, "Hell, she's probably there already."

Vladimir thought, "If I were a hawk, how long, over how many miles could I soar before, growing weary, I put my talons down on the land?"

In his head he heard the echo of a poem, and in his mind's eye he saw a "… *dapple-dawn drawn Falcon, in his riding*
Of the rolling level underneath him steady air, and striding
High there, how he rung upon the rein of a wimpling wing
In his ecstasy! Then off, off forth on swing … ."

"Were I a falcon, could I ride the steady air, could I follow the Hudson all the way up into the mountains until the river narrows into a stream, then a skip-across brook, then a mere trickle from a tiny spring? Could I go that far on wimpling wing? Perhaps, if the wind were right and stayed under me, perhaps I could soar forever. No, that's impossible; nothing is forever. But, then, how do we know how long 'forever' is, especially to a hawk? What about a mayfly that lives for just a day? A whole lifetime in just one day. Perhaps forever can be just an afternoon or just a summer evening. Or one, or the other."

Alas, regardless of their doom,
The little victims play!
No sense have they of ills to come,
Nor care beyond today
　　　　　— From *On a Distant Prospect of*
　　　　　Eton College by Thomas Gray

Constance, a girl named Mary, and Vladimir were holding hands, strolling along the walkway atop the Croton Dam, a historic three-hundred-foot-high structure of hewn granite. On one side, looking down over the railing, they could see the spillway, a terraced apron of large stepped stones over which the water falls. It shattered into foam, re-gathered itself, then calmed into a riffled stream and flowed on to its rendezvous with the Hudson and the sea.

Looking over the other side of the parapet, they could see, hunched tight against the face of the dam, the accumulated waters of the Croton River (the Indians called it the Kitchawan), which begins as a trickle from a spring a hundred miles north high up in the Pawling Mountains. It was more than a hundred years ago, during the 1830s and '40s that this dam was built to interrupt the river's journey to the Hudson. Now, behind the dam's broad granite shoulders a vast reservoir stood, holding thirty-four billion gallons of impatient water awaiting its turn to escape through a great, complex system of aqueducts built back then to quench Manhattan's thirst with the pure clean water of this little river.

There are some things that must be pent up and held back, like vicious dogs and madmen. Like the fulfillment of obsessions. And, if we need water, pure and clean, then little rivers must be held back to create great reservoirs to quench our thirst.

"Vladimir, what's a dam for?" asked Mary.

"Well, as you can see, to hold the water back and make a reservoir."

"Why do they want to hold the water back?"

"Because we need water to drink and bathe and wash our Jaguars and our linens. How else would we get the strawberry jam off our cheeks?"

"Oh, but there's water everywhere and it doesn't seem fair to hold back this little river just because we have cars and linens and our little mouths to wash." Mary pouted.

"Well, I suppose there are bigger reasons than that, Mary. Or perhaps that is reason enough."

"Does the water like being held back?" asked Constance.

"I'm not sure. I don't think I've ever thought of that. Let's see. I don't suppose it does, but, well, look there across the reservoir. It does seem calm and contented."

"But how about down there?" Mary was pointing to the spillway beneath them. "That water doesn't look very contented to me. Looks like the water can't wait to get out of the reservoir."

"Well, you're right about that. The water down there does appear, well, angry, boisterous, out of control. Very eager, I'd say, to escape the reservoir. So you may be right. I don't suppose the water really likes being held back."

"Boisterous? What does 'boisterous' mean?" Mary asked.

"Well, boisterous means nasty, rowdy, uncontrollable. Like boys at school. Everything that little girls are not."

"Has this dam been here forever?" asked Constance.

"Of course not. God makes rivers; men build dams."

"Then has the river been here forever?"

"Perhaps."

"Now that the dam is here, will it be here forever?"

"Well, Constance, forever is a very, very long time—longer than one can even imagine—and the dam has been here already for a very long time, and it will, I think, be here for yet another very long time. But 'forever,' I am not so sure."

"Well, the pyramids, they have been there forever," said Mary.

"Now they're all fallen down, aren't they?" said Constance.

"They are not. That's not so," said Mary. "And I suppose they have not really been there forever either."

"But what if the Croton dam were to fall down? Then we'd all be in trouble," said Constance.

"You mean what if it burst?" said Mary, looking down at the stones and mortar under her feet and prancing on her tiptoes as if she were walking across red-hot coals.

"Oh, then we would be in *deep* trouble, "Constance laughed at what she thought was a good joke. "The boisterous waters would wash away the whole village, the church, the school, oh, *the school*, and Mr. Carnaby's drugstore, everything."

"Constance, stop it. That's scary." Mary tugged at Vladimir's hand.

"Would it really wash everything away?" Mary looked up at Vladimir.

"Yes, I'm afraid if it burst it really might."

"Most especially *the school*, the whole Cortlandt Elementary School, right, Vladimir?" said Constance giggling.

"Most especially the school."

"Yippee! Yippee!" Both the little girls leaped up and down and screamed.

Then Constance said, "Well, I suppose that's because the waters are angry for having been pent up and held back for all these years in the reservoir. They would be taking revenge on the people who pent them up. My mother says it's bad to store up your anger. Or, as she says, 'to pent up your emotions.'"

"Oh, yes," said Mary, "that's *not* good. The more you do that the more trouble you are in for. And, like, well, a million-million gazillion angry lions, tigers, and bears the water would rush out and devour the village just to get even."

"But why us? The angry waters should kill all the New Yorkers, not us. We don't drink that water. They do. Not us. It's only fair that they spare us and wash away all the thirsty New Yorkers instead." Constance had solved the problem.

"My conclusion is this," Constance released Vladimir's hand and stood with her hands on her hips. "This dam is dangerous. But dangerous to the wrong people. And I don't like the idea of dangerous dams, much less 'angry' water waiting to devour me and wash me away."

"Ladies, here is what we have established: This dam is a mean thing, but only from the river's point of view, because it prevents the waters of the Croton River from doing what they want to do—running and leaping, doing pirouettes, pliés, and grand jetés all the way down to the Hudson—and that makes the water angry and that's what makes the whole thing dangerous. Because pent up water like pent up emotions can be very destructive. But, then, we know that dams like this can last as long as the pyramids, and they are certainly more practical than pyramids. So, my little darlings, I think in a practical sense, this dam may not really be such a bad thing. We need things like this in the world to keep other things from doing exactly what they want to do. After all we cannot have everyone and everything doing exactly what they want to do, like driving on the wrong side of the street."

"What's that got to do with dams?" said Mary.

"Here's what. If we could do whatever we wanted to do whenever we wanted to do it, we might hurt other people, right, Vladimir?" Constance stood again, arms akimbo.

"Right. We need things to hold us back."

"But who would want to do that, to hurt other people?" said Mary.

"Lots of people," said Vladimir. "You know that."

"Evil people," said Constance. "And there are lots and lots of those."

"But don't we put evil people in prisons?" Asked Mary. "Isn't that what prisons are for?"

"But not all evil people are in prison. Only those who get caught. So I don't understand. The water isn't evil, it isn't even angry until it gets pent up in the reservoir," said Constance.

"Things like this are always different … but the same. And the prison is, in a way, the same as the reservoir—the dam—because it 'pens up' evil people, and prevents them from harming other people," said Vladimir. "And that's very interesting, Constance, because if the prison down in Ossining were to burst and all the evil, angry people were to break out, just as if the dam burst, then people would get hurt, maybe even killed because all those evil people could then do exactly what they wanted to do. And since they are in prison because they stole things from people, hurt people, and killed people, we know if they got loose that's what they'd continue to do."

"Oh, how frightening," said Mary.

"Now ladies, ladies, it is a beautiful day and you mustn't be frightened of anything especially such things as dams and prisons, angry water, and evil people. The water is not evil, perhaps it gets evil … no, let's just say it only gets dangerous when you pen it up behind a dam. Or better said, 'potentially' dangerous. But then dams and prisons don't often burst."

"Constance, you said your Mommy says that 'pent-up desires' are bad for you," said Mary. "I think that's what makes people's faces break out."

"Ooooo, now that's a thought. What if those waters were all our 'pent-up desires' crouching behind the dam. Ooooo, Vladimir just think of that. Then if the dam burst we would all be washed away with desire," Constance laughed and squeezed his hand.

"Well, like it or not, there must be things like dams, and prisons, things like rules and laws to hold back all the forces that might harm us. Yes, even our pent-up desires. Holding things back *can* be dangerous. Think of a rubber band. Left alone it's harmless but pull it back, release it, and it can sting. The boys at the dump use big rubber bands to make their slingshots to kill the rats. So many things, well, almost anything can become dangerous. A stick isn't dangerous until someone picks it up and hits you on the head with it.

"This doesn't mean that you should be afraid of things. Then you'd become little 'fraidy cats.' Afraid to go out of the house, afraid to go to ballet school, afraid to ride in a car, afraid to stand here on this dam. Yes, I suppose there really are things lurking all around us that might hurt us. But, because most of them—no, practically all of them—are, well, you know, under control, we need not fear them."

"Oh, Vladimir, we are so lucky aren't we, to have you to protect us from such evil things as angry water, rubber bands, sticks, and, ooo, ooo, ooo, most especially our pent up desires." Constance and Mary threw their heads back, puckered their lips, spread their arms and danced a circle around Vladimir, singing "ooo, ooo, ooo, ooo, ooo, ooo."

April is the cruelest month, breeding
Lilacs out of the dead land, mixing
Memory and desire, stirring
Dull roots with spring rain.
— From *The Waste Land*, opening lines,
Part I. Burial of The Dead, by T. S. Eliot

Constance Carmichael disappeared on one of those early April days when wet winds scurry out of the northeast, making lilac buds shiver in their gusts; when the sun hides like a reading lamp lit beneath bed covers of rumpled purple clouds; and when the new, bright green grass grows restless under the chiaroscuro sky.

If you lived in Croton on such a day in the encirclement of homes close to the village center, you could easily stroll down to the village shops. So it was not unusual for children to be permitted by even the most attentive and protective parents to stroll down to Carnaby's Drugstore on errands to pick up, say, a tube of Pepsodent or to drop off Daddy's shoes for a pair of new heels at Palermo's.

The Carmichaels lived in the encirclement. It was a walk to the drugstore from which Constance never returned.

Constance's mother, Elizabeth Carmichael, had dark brown eyes as lustrous as French-polished walnut. They were so dark, in fact, the pupils were indistinguishable from the irises. Her hair, which matched her eyes in color and luster, was pulled back into a ponytail held by an apple-red scrunchie. She had the oval face and liquid slenderness of a woman in a Modigliani painting. Her lips, untouched by lipstick, were the color of rosé wine. She was busy in the kitchen preparing dinner that late afternoon—sautéed chicken breasts with apricots, a splash of bourbon and pecans—when Constance asked to go to Carnaby's.

"Sure, sure, go ahead. But don't be gone long," she said distractedly without turning from her task.

"Want anything, Mom?"

"No, sweetheart, nothing."

Being busy in the kitchen, she did not miss her daughter for an hour or more. When she did, she wiped her hands on her apron and went to the front door. Constance's yellow slicker was gone. It had been hanging on one of the umbrellas in the stand by the door. Her little yellow slicker hat was gone too.

Elizabeth opened the front door and walked onto the porch. She wore a dark blue sweater over a ribbed cashmere turtleneck. And khaki pants. She was sock-less in penny loafers. She stood with her hands on her hips just outside the front door. The chilly breeze tugged at her khakis pushing them tight against her thighs. She stood there motionless until the chill began to nibble at her bare ankles. Then she went inside.

Once inside an immense feeling of desolation spread over her like poured paint. She flushed and pressed her palms to her cheeks, then ran her hands through her hair. Her neck flushed under the turtleneck. She went back to the front door, looked at the umbrella stand again. Then she looked outside pressing her face tightly to the front door's windowpane. The world outside appeared to be desolate, a gray, wet, cold, inhospitable place where the only living thing was the wind. A wind that rubbed its brutish back against the siding of the Carmichaels' house and moaned.

"Constance … Constance!" Elizabeth whispered before she turned and called up the stairs. "Constance, are you up there?" There was no answer. All she could hear was the sound of the wind.

Her face and neck flushed again. She hooked her fingers in the turtleneck and pulled it back from her neck. Then she went to the telephone and called Carnaby's.

"Grace? Oh, hello, Grace. This is Elizabeth, Elizabeth Carmichael. Have you seen Constance? I mean did Constance come in there, is she there now? She went down there to pick something up—oh, I, I don't even remember what it was. She didn't say. She's been gone for well over an hour. Have you seen her?"

Grace had not seen her.

"Well, call me back, will you, please, if you do?" After she hung up, she felt a helix of panic spiral like a whirlwind through her body. To steady herself, she bent over and gripped both sides of the telephone stand. "Sarah, that's it, Sarah," she thought, "maybe she stopped off at Sarah's house on the way back. Yes, of course. That's what she's done."

Again she reached for the telephone. There was no answer at Sarah's. For a moment she felt like Dorothy, her home swept up in the spiral of a Kansas tornado. She stood there in a dizzying vortex of confusion, terror, and fear. "Stop it," she whispered to herself. "Stop it." She looked at the ceiling and then the clock. It was five thirty. "Calm down. Be calm."

The closet. Why hadn't she thought of that? She came home and hung up her coat and hat and went upstairs. She opened the closet looking again for Constance's raincoat. No, that's not likely. She would have said something. She always said, "Hello, Mom, I'm home, going upstairs." The coat wasn't there.

She walked to the bottom of the stairs, "Constance, are you up there?" she yelled.

She wasn't upstairs. So Elizabeth turned again to the closet, reached for her trench coat and slipped it over her shoulders. The wooden hanger clattered to the floor. "I'll just walk down to the drugstore. Walk. Not run." She urged herself to be calm. "I'd better look upstairs first just to make sure. Maybe she's napping."

She turned again and walked to the foot of the stairs. She was afraid to go up. "Constance! Constance! Answer me. Constance, sweetheart, are you up there?" she called out. "Maybe she's in the shower, running the water, and she can't hear me. That's it. I just didn't hear her come home." She placed her hand on the balustrade, then she looked back at the front door. "I wonder why Grace didn't see her? Well, I suppose that's possible," she thought. "She was probably busy somewhere else. In the back of the store. No, it isn't possible. Carnaby's is too small for that. For Christ's sake Grace is the cashier. She would have seen her. But if Constance bought something, she would have had to be there to ring it up. Well, that's OK, that's OK now. That's OK. She just hasn't gotten to the drugstore; that explains it. Maybe it wasn't a whole hour after all. She probably stopped off at Sarah's—no, they didn't answer their telephone. Well, then, she stopped to talk to friends. She—how many times have I told her not to do that? I've told her a thousand times not to do that—not to hang out on the corner. That's where she is, on the corner yakking with the boys. But on a chilly day like this?" She cinched the belt of the trench coat tightly around her waist and opened the front door.

"How horrible it is out here," she thought. "How utterly bleak. Feels more like March than April."

There was no one on the corner. The pavement was deserted. It looked like an abandoned town in a movie set. No one, not a single person was on the street. Had it been a Friday, when the men and women who work in the city take the early train home, the street would have been filled with cars—wives going down to pick up their husbands. But it was Thursday. Late Thursday afternoon.

She walked into Carnaby's. "Grace, you haven't seen Constance?" She tried to appear calm and casual. "She came down here to pick up something—I can't remember what the devil it was. But it was about an hour ago."

"I told you when you called. No, Liz, I haven't seen her." Grace sensed the urgency in Elizabeth's voice and there was a quiver in her own voice.

"What's the matter? Has something happened?"

"No, of course not. Nothing. Nothing's *happened*."

"But you seem upset. Look, Liz, she just stopped off somewhere. That's all. You know how kids are. Did you check with any of her friends?"

"Yes, I called Sarah's house but no answer."

"Well, let's look outside." She touched Elizabeth's sleeve and then turned her head toward the back of the store. "George! George! I'm just going outside, out front, for just a minute." Grace took hold of Elizabeth's arm as the two stepped out into the deserted street.

Paul Carmichael came home on the seven-thirty train, and when he got there, he found Elizabeth in tears. "What's happened? Calm down, Liz. Please, calm down. Tell me what's happened, darling."

"Paul, nothing, nothing. It's just that Constance went to the drugstore, hours ago. She hasn't come back. I called Sarah's and she's not there; I mean there's no answer there."

"Calm down, Liz. For God's sake, there's no reason to panic"

"I am not panicking, Paul. I'm just concerned."

"Alright, alright."

"Paul, what's happened? Where can she be?"

"It will be alright, Liz. Everything will be alright." He felt as if his insides had been scooped out—he felt hollow, empty, as hollow, light, and fragile as a Christmas-tree ornament. He felt fear. He thought thoughts that he never wished to think. They bubbled up with a chilly effervescence from the bottom of his emptiness, and try as he might, he could not push them down. Then vivid memories of Constance, like shards from a broken mirror, glittered helter-skelter through his consciousness. This cannot, cannot be happening. God, oh please God, tell me this is not happening. He reached for the telephone.

Man produces evil as a bee produces honey.
— From a 1962 speech by William Golding,
author of *Lord of The Flies*

Croton-on-Hudson, population seventy-five hundred, founded in 1797, is a historic village within the town of Cortlandt, New York, seven miles north of the Tappan Zee Bridge in Tarrytown— Washington Irving country. Croton sits benignly on the river's edge thirty-three miles north of Manhattan. Its main street back then was the Old Albany Post Road, now it's Route 9, which meanders from Manhattan through all the Hudson River towns, including Croton and on up to Peekskill and beyond.

In the early days, as it passed through Croton, the Old Albany Post Road was called Riverside Avenue. Back then this was the commercial center of the village, and Riverside Avenue was its main street. It was lined with several little shops, all of which were demolished in the 1960s to make room for the construction of a four-lane bypass. Today, the commercial center of the village lies up the hill along a remnant of old Route 9 within sight of the river. Nothing more, as it was then, but a string of little shops.

Once a summertime retreat for well-heeled New Yorkers, Croton-on-Hudson is now principally a village of commuters, men in gray and dark blue pinstriped suits from Brooks Brother's who are taxied every morning to the station from their homes in the hills by their sleepy-eyed wives, and left off in the turn-around at the Croton-Harmon station to board the New York Central trains that will take them to their jobs in the city as publishers, editors, television producers, financial analysts, bond traders, brokers, artists.

They are the educated, privileged intelligentsias, politically liberal, and avant-garde Democrats. In their own minds, they were masters of the universe.

And then there are the descendants of the Italian workmen who came to Croton in the 1840s to build the dam: stonecutters, masons, and carpenters. They lived in the row houses down the hill closer to the river.

In the 1840s there were several prominent—politically prominent, that is—Italian families living in Croton. The most powerful patriarch of one of these families was John "Big John" Gagliardi. He was called "Mr. Republican." And when plans for the dam were completed, the contractors came to him and asked him to write home and invite relatives to come across the Atlantic to help build the dam. At home, in Italy, the wage at the time was fifty cents a day. Work on the dam paid considerably more than that. So word spread and eventually nearly one hundred of them came to Croton.

Under Gagliardi's influence they became naturalized citizens and joined the Republican Party. They voted the way Big John suggested, and, therefore, not only built the dam but also built Big John's political power base. By nature they were politically conservative. Catholics. To add to their social cohesion, they had come, nearly all of them, from Cosenza, Italy, a village south of Salerno along the costal highway, a place where the fields, never defiled by snow, are bright green and spread out from the white beaches of the Mediterranean's Tyrrhenian Sea inland like carefully folded cloth.

Among these immigrants was John, patriarch of the Corsetti family. He was a stonecutter and became a lieutenant in the army of skilled workmen who labored on the dam for ten years and more.

These were strong, powerful men who brought with them equally strong, supportive, and determined women. It was as if, as the men shaped the stones, the stones shaped them. And their women, too. It was as if the strength of the stones flowed into them as they breathed the granite dust, as if granite dust mixed with the blood in their veins. These were granite-muscled men with square chests and broad shoulders. Men as hard as blocks of granite. Their women were the mortar of their lives.

They lived then and now in the lower part of the village within sight of the marina in redbrick row houses with white-spindled porches and three-step stone stoops. The houses were built especially for them along the narrow streets of lower Croton by the contractors building the dam. The descendants of these cutters, now with no stone cutting left to do except for the few stone houses occasionally built for wealthy residents, worked in the railroad shops and yards opened by John Harmon in 1913. To this day, in the great yards, in the sheds and roundhouse, the New York Central's Hudson Division repairs and cleans passenger cars and locomotives, preparing them for their daily runs down to Manhattan—first stop south, Ossining—and back up to Croton again.

Back then, as now, the Croton-Harmon station was a busy place where you could catch excursion trains coming up from Manhattan. The Adirondack Express took passengers from Manhattan to Montreal in a day; the Ethan Allen carried leaf-peepers up to Vermont in the fall; and the Empire Express's destination was Niagara Falls. The more business-oriented runs carrying salesmen overnight to such picturesque destinations as Buffalo, Rochester and Syracuse was fondly called the Willie Loman Express by aficionados of the train who Scotched themselves up in the bar car, squeezed into roomettes, and rumbled off through the night to destinations that some said were on the very edge of the earth.

On weekday mornings the descendants of the sons of Cosenza would grab their black lunch boxes, spill out of their row homes, trickle down toward the river's edge, and cross the tracks to their jobs in the Harmon yards. Except for Croton's bright river-town patina, this scene would remind one of the gaggles of workers shuffling off to the mines in a Thomas Hardy novel.

Of course, not all the Corsenzans worked in the yards. Some were now contractors and carpenters. Cops and firemen. Among these was one Angelo Corsetti, third generation Cosenzan born in Croton. He had his father's broad, square shoulders, big hands, blue eyes, and black hair. His father's short, thick legs. Even his father's thick black Fuller-brush moustache. He was a graduate of Croton-Harmon High School, where he played football, and of the State University of New York at New Paltz, where he majored in criminal justice with a minor in business administration. Now he was Croton's Chief of Police, a job he had held for four years now. This meant he was an expert at rousting preppy kids out of the park below the dam, out of the old cemetery up the hill, and enforcing the noise ordinance plus signing gun permits for his pals in the Croton Rod and Gun Club.

When Paul Carmichael called the Croton police station at 8:30 pm that Thursday evening, he spoke with Sergeant Palermo, who then relayed the contents of the call to Chief Corsetti at his home.

"Hey, Angelo, just got a call from Paul Carmichael. Looks like we have a missing child: Constance Carmichael. She's eleven; lives on Sunnyside Drive. Been missing for, well, best estimate, four or five hours. The parents have checked with friends. No luck. She was last seen by her mother, Elizabeth, just before the little girl went down to Carnaby's to pick up something at around, oh, 4:30 pm. The mother's not quite sure of the time."

As he listened to Palermo, Corsetti thought, "OK, a missing kid. A little girl. Only eleven. Doesn't happen often around here, and when it does, it is usually no big deal. It's usually resolved in a few hours, a day at most." He remembered once there was that smart-ass Northfield kid, Jonathan, who stole fifty bucks from his mother's purse and bought himself a one-way ticket to Manhattan. The NYPD found him the next morning sleeping on a bench in Grand Central Station. They put him up in a cell at the precinct house for the rest of the night, and P. J. O'Malley, a retired NYPD detective who lives in Croton, escorted him home on the train the next day. The kid thought it was a pretty cool adventure. Of course, there'd be kids who decided to sleep over at a friend's house and forget to call their folks. They'd always find them the next day. No big deal.

Corsetti knew the routine. But this was not some smart-ass high school kid. This was a little girl. Even so, they would first need a very detailed description of Constance: what she was wearing, the color of her hair, height, weight, and age. A photograph. Palermo had got most of this information over the telephone from Paul Carmichael. He had sent a patrolman—Croton had two on duty that night—over to the Carmichael's to pick up the photograph.

If she had not been found by morning, Corsetti himself would go over to interview the parents to get more detailed information on the little girl, her family, friends, habits—all that. But this could wait until morning. Tonight the two Croton patrolmen would keep an eye out for the girl, scout around the village. The police departments in the other towns along the river would immediately be alerted to do the same. So the call went out: Croton has a missing girl. Description follows. Then as soon as they had it, they would fax her picture to them. Corsetti also told Palermo to alert the state police and the F.B.I.

Corsetti had zero experience with the real thing. A real disappearance. Maybe textbook knowledge, yes, but no first-hand experience in handling the real thing himself. Of course, at around 9:30 Thursday night, given his past experience, there was probably little reason to believe that this was, in fact, the real thing. But if it did turn out to be a real missing persons case, he'd need some help.

After his call from Palermo, Corsetti hung up and went to the refrigerator for a bottle of Budweiser and a piece of salami. At the moment, he had the place to himself. Mary and the girls had gone shopping in White Plains. He'd be able to watch the third game of the playoffs undisturbed.

While he watched the game, Corsetti thought of P. J. O'Malley, his old pal and fellow member of the Croton Rod and Gun Club. If there were even a hint that this was the real thing, he'd call Patrick. He'd call him anyway. He'd know exactly what to do. But unless Patrick happened to call tonight to comment on the score of the game, he'd wait until tomorrow. He'd wait until the afternoon.

A sudden blow: the great wings beating still
Above the staggering girl, her thighs caressed
By the dark webs, her nape caught in the bill,
He holds her helpless breast upon his breast.
— From *Leda and the Swan*
by William Butler Yeats

W hen he got up on Friday morning, Corsetti called the Carmichael's from his home and arranged to stop by and interview them before going to the office.

By three o'clock, Corsetti was worried. There was still no sign of Constance. This was beginning to look like abduction. A kidnapping. And the disappearance of a child—all disappearances—required a waiting period of forty-eight hours before such cases are given official missing-person status. This meant that there was twenty-four hours left to wait and see. He had no choice but to follow normal routine.

It would be Saturday before the forty-eight-hour missing-person criteria had been met. But he couldn't wait that long. Right now he had no choice but to believe that Constance was kidnapped, a word he would never use in front of the parents. She was a child under the age of eighteen.

She was now assumed to be in danger of serious bodily harm or death, and as a result of his initial investigation he believed that the abduction was committed by a non-family member.

Back at the office he put the routine wheels in motion. After several cups of coffee, he called O'Malley.

"Patrick, I've got a little problem. I need to pick your brains. Looks like we've got a missing child. And it looks like a kidnapping."

"What? Right here in Croton? Who is it?"

"I don't have time right now to give you the details. Just come over, let's say, after four. OK? Right. See you then. Thanks"

At half past noon, another alert went out with more detailed information on the victim. By 1:00 pm the victim's information was patched into a statewide alert and an additional dispatch was sent directly to the New York State Police. All the necessary paperwork now lay on his desk. Not much left to do but sit by the telephone and wait for P. J. O'Malley to arrive.

Man is a slayer by instinct ... that rarity in nature, an animal which will kill for pleasure.
  — From the tetralogy, *The Once and Future King,*
  The Book of Merlyn by T. H. White

If you could not guess it by the name, the lilt of a brogue would give it away: Patrick Joseph O'Malley was born on the "other side, " meaning the other side of the Atlantic Ocean, in the town of Clonmel in Tipperary, in the center of what is called Ireland's Golden Vale, celebrated as the greenest spot on the Emerald Isle, which, of course, would make it the greenest spot on the face of God's green earth.

His father, Thomas Aloysius O'Malley, like many in that time and place lived an impoverished life. So when he reached his teens, to help support his family Thomas enlisted in the British Army, a practice that, although fairly common, was locally frowned upon; yet, it was one of the few ways that a son of Ireland could help to support his mother, father, sisters, and brothers. So Thomas joined the British Army and every month sent his pay straight home to his mother.

When he returned from the army, he married his childhood sweetheart, Katherine Marie McNulty, and got a job in a nearby rock quarry. As P.J.

would tell his son, Danny, "My dad, your granddad, he got a job at the quarry making little ones out of big ones."

Among the quarrymen the standard technique for toughening one's hands to protect them from the hot bite of the pick axe handle was to soak them in salt water and then rub them with salt. Now most of them could afford the salt but Thomas and his fellow rock splitters couldn't afford the salt, so, as Patrick explained to his son, "My dad, he and the other poor boys, why what they'd do is they'd piss on their hands to salt them up."

By 1928 Thomas A. O'Malley had four children. Patrick, born in 1923, was five years old. And it was that year when Thomas had a bit of good luck—well, more like hard-earned yet unexpected good fortune.

Clonmel was a town through which three rivers ran—a town of bridges. Despite all the water, most of the Clonmel men at that time couldn't swim. Thomas was among the few who could. He had learned in the British Army. Now one day a carriage was clattering across one of these narrow, arched stone bridges when the horses reared and the wheels spun on the slippery stones. The carriage swerved, crashed into the side of the bridge, flipped over, and as quick as the telling dumped its contents—the driver, a woman, and her three small children—into the river.

The hand of divine providence, as Patrick tells the story, had placed Thomas and another man, a stranger, on the very same bridge that day at the moment of the crash. Both men, Tom and the stranger, immediately dove into the water—by coincidence or, again, by providence the stranger also knew how to swim. Together, they managed to pull the driver, the woman, and all the children to the safety of the river's bank. But it was a bitterly cold, rainy day, and one of the children and the driver, a man in his seventies, later died of pneumonia. Tom suffered from the chill and lay abed for four days. The stranger was never heard from again.

A month later Ireland's Humane Society—which in Ireland concerns itself with humans not animals—heard about Tom's heroic deed and gave him a reward—the sum of fifty pounds and a framed certificate of valor. With his prize in hand, Thomas told Katherine that he was buying a ticket for passage to America. He would leave the green fields of Ireland for the gritty streets of New York. When he'd found work there and saved enough money, he'd send for her and the children.

Thus, Thomas Aloysius O'Malley ended up in Yorkville in the heart of the Bronx. Herbert Hoover, a Republican, had just been elected president; Amelia Earhart had just flown across the Atlantic; Jack Sharkey was the new heavyweight champion. To Thomas it seemed like another world, and, indeed, another world it was, a gray, dirty, and bustling world, a galaxy away from the emerald fields and hardscrabble poverty he knew in Clonmel.

Thomas moved into a dingy railroad flat, which he shared with fifteen other Irish immigrants. He found work as a "hustler," the name for baggage handlers, downtown at the Biltmore Hotel, and within eight months he had earned enough American dollars to send five steerage-class tickets to Katherine.

Before his family arrived, Thomas had managed to find a better-paying job at Power House One on the Lower East Side. When the stock market crashed and the Great Depression began in 1929, Thomas, unlike thousands of others, kept his job, but his salary was cut to the bone. He had barely enough to feed his family, let alone pay the rent. So his strategy in those years was to move every three months since the custom was for a landlord to rent an apartment with the understanding that the first two months would be free—if the tenant agreed to pay for the third month up front. So when the third month came and went, the Thomas O'Malley's would pack up their belongings in cardboard boxes and move.

Patrick would never forget those peripatetic days, and once when he saw his son Danny packing cardboard boxes to go away to college, he actually wept. "What's wrong, Dad?" said Danny. So Patrick told Danny the story of those early years in Yorkville.

"Danny, promise me, promise me, don't ever pack up your things in those Chinese suitcases and leave this house for good."

Danny said, "I won't, Dad; I'll be back."

At first, the Thomas O'Malley's lived on the Upper East Side on the corner of 96th Street and York Avenue in the South Bronx. Then they moved to Eagle Avenue and Tinton also in the South Bronx. In that apartment building there lived a man named Hayes who was in the business of smuggling drugs out of Turkey. He was a tall man, over six feet four with curly blonde hair. As Patrick O'Malley remembered, "He was a handsome dog of a man, yes, indeed, he was." Knowing this man was a genuine brush with fame because "he's the chap," Patrick would tell Danny, "that the book *The Midnight Express* was based on." Patrick relished the story.

The Yorkville area of the South Bronx is perhaps as scruffy now as it was then when all the thugs doing stick-ups and burglaries were young Irish immigrants. Patrick himself almost fell into a life of thuggery just before the summer of 1939. He was sixteen at the time, and with his best friend Tommy Hines and a German kid named Hans Bohr, they decided to pull a caper of their own. They knew this guy who was making cash pickups—a money-runner, not a banker—in the old 4-5 uptown, an area now known as Fort Apache. They planned to ambush him, steal his sack, and disappear in the crowd. They rehearsed every detail over and over again. But when the time came to pull the caper, they all lost their nerve.

At his father's urging, Patrick joined the Civilian Conservation Corps, a kind of boot camp for young men. He was shipped all the way out west to Brigham City, Utah, and worked that summer as a bricklayer's apprentice building a government school for Indians.

In the winter of 1940, when he turned seventeen, he asked his mother for permission to join the army—you needed your parent's permission to join if you were under eighteen. A street-tough city kid, Patrick was placed among a group of Apple Knockers, the name for country boys, from Cohoes, Clifton Park, and Watervillette, all spots in upstate New York north of Albany known as apple country.

He spent five and a half years in the army, mostly in Hawaii. At twenty-one, in 1944, he found himself in the sixty-day-long Battle of Saipan. Tommy Hines was killed in that battle. Patrick's only wounds were received the night after he serendipitously ran across his brother Mike scavenging the battlefield for swords to take home as souvenirs. That night he and Mike celebrated their unexpected reunion by getting drunk. Patrick recalled that as the night Mike "knocked the stuffins outa me."

Patrick was promoted and busted several times. Once, for example, when on his watch, thirteen cases of beer mysteriously disappeared from the PX. He was called on the carpet. In his defense, he said, "Hell, Sergeant, that wasn't that much beer. And it wasn't stolen. We just drank it." His truthfulness cost him his stripes.

When he came home from the army, he got a job at Penn Station working for the Pennsylvania Railroad. It lasted only for a couple of months. Then he worked for the USPS That lasted six months. Then at the age of twenty-four, he decided to become a cop. In the Battle of Saipan he was on one of the ships that encircled the island in preparation for the bombardment. When it started, he was on deck under one of the big guns, and the first shot popped both his eardrums. As a result he lost 70 percent of the hearing in one ear and 30 percent in the other. Normally, being disabled was problematic, but in Patrick's case it got him several more points on the exam, and they overlooked his disability. In December 1947, Patrick J. O'Malley became a New York City police officer.

After ten years on the beat, his best friend, Frankie Banks, one of the seven elite plainclothes detectives assigned to the Bronx—a plum job secured on the basis of one's connections within the department—asked Patrick if he wanted in. Patrick said yes. "Well, first," Banks explained, "you have to pass muster with the captain. Do you play golf?" asked Frankie. "Yeah," lied Patrick. So Frankie arranged for the captain and Patrick to play a game of golf at Van Cortlandt Park. They hit it off, and Patrick was inducted into the ranks of the elite plainclothes investigators in the Bronx.

Frankie had told him that it was a rotation system, which meant that he got three years in as an investigator. Three years, no more. After that it was somebody else's turn. Since the jobs were supposed to be like tenured professorships, to move a guy out they had to "make up trouble." That's the way it worked. That was the deal. No one complained. You agreed to that setup in the beginning. So at the end of Patrick's three-year stint, they "made up trouble", said he was sleeping on the job, some cockamamie thing like that and his plum job as an investigator ended.

He had become a member of the elite seven in 1957 and was "rotated" out in 1960. When it was over the captain asked him, "Patrick, where do you want to go now?" O'Malley said that he wanted to go to someplace where he didn't have to climb up and down those damn stairs. So the benevolent captain assigned him to the vast, level expanse of the notorious 4-5.

In the summer of 1960, he was married and living on Fordham Road at University Avenue. One day his wife, Mary, saw a disheveled lady tottering across University Avenue. She was, for God's sake, dressed in nothing more than a flannel bathrobe and bedroom slippers. To Mary that signaled that the shanty Irish had invaded their neighborhood. They had to move. This time they really moved—thirty-three miles upriver to the village of Croton-on-Hudson where they bought the little Swiss chalet at 62 Morningside Drive. They moved there on January 27, 1961, during a blizzard. And O'Malley became a commuter, rubbing shoulders with the other Crotonites on the daily 7:37 to Grand Central Station.

During his tenure on the NYPD, P. J. O'Malley rose to the rank of detective. Now he was retired with a nice pension. He even had a little place down in St. Petersburg where he often spent January, February, and March. Fishing mostly. After Mary died he held onto their little home on Morningside Drive. It was a home stuffed with memories. The front porch and the yard were always cluttered with Patrick's many unfinished projects, much to the annoyance of his neighbors. It had been their home for thirty years, and the current neighbors said that they thought the paint buckets and brushes had been there on the porch railing for at least that long, if not longer.

Patrick loved the summers there. He loved to sit on the porch, smoke cigarettes, read the *New York Times* and the *Croton-Harmon News* and listen to the Croton River flow by—the house was that close to the banks of the river. He loved to fly fish in the upper Croton below the dam, which was stocked regularly with trout. He would come up from Florida in late March to get prepared for opening day on April 1. What's more, he enjoyed spending time with his son, Danny, and daughter, Marie. Danny now had an engineering degree from Plattsburgh State College and Marie had a Masters in English lit from Columbia University. Patrick, who was mostly self-educated with some night school thrown in, had never gone to college, and he wore his children's academic success as a badge of honor more proudly than he ever wore his NYPD gold.

O'Malley was six foot two, lanky, loosely put together with curly salt and pepper hair. He had about him the air and manner of a man very much at home in the world. People who watched the old movies on TV said he looked like that old-time movie star Robert Ryan. He was, no doubt about it, the genuine article. He brought his brogue from Ireland and mixed it with a New York City twang. He always had a smile on his face and a story to tell. He made it a point to read every book on the *New York Times* bestseller list, fiction and non-fiction alike—"Once you catch up," he said," it ain't really all that hard." He wore his considerable, self-acquired learning as loosely as his clothes. There wasn't a subject that Patrick Joseph O'Malley couldn't talk about. Intelligently.

His manners and appearance did not calculate to please;
His coat was torn and seedy, he was baggy at the knees;
One ear was somewhat missing, no need to tell you why,
And he scowled upon a hostile world from one forbidding eye.
— From *Old Possum's Book of Practical Cats*
by T.S. Eliot

W earing his dark blue New York Yankees baseball cap, khaki shirt, and boot-cut jeans, O'Malley drove his Chevy wagon over to the police station late in the afternoon on Friday. Now he was sitting in the chief's office.

After he looked at the papers on Corsetti's desk, O'Malley rubbed his chin and said, "Maybe this does look like an abduction." He leaned forward and put his elbows on the desk, making a bridge with his fingers to rest his chin on. "A mysterious disappearance, which means, pal, ya gotta suspect abduction, nasty as that sounds. And even nastier, ya gotta suspect—especially as time passes—even the possibility of murder. But so far all we've got is a missing little girl. Just missing overnight. That's all, but it's enough. And ya gotta expect the worst."

"You're right, Patrick. But for Christ's sake, this is Croton, not New

York City. And this is not a murder. Not yet anyway. It's, well, OK a disappearance. Hell, not even that yet. Not really. She's just missing. That's for sure. Now help me figure out how the hell to deal with this?"

"Look, Jimmy, girls—little girls and big ones—they disappear everyday, and many, well, unfortunately, many are never found. The average person can't imagine how many little girls—and little boys, too—disappear, without a trace, and never ever show up again. Yes, in small towns as well as big cities. Many of these cases don't turn out to be murders; they are mysterious disappearances. And they stay that way. Unsolved. You must know the statistics. They're horrendous."

O'Malley sat back in the chair, spread his legs, and put his hands on top of his head. "Everyone knows there are, 'sexual predators,' lots of them out there. They prey almost exclusively on little girls. Little boys, too. They see a kid, stalk 'em, and nab 'em. We got to assume that's what might have happened here."

"You're right," said Corsetti. "This is a small town. She'd have showed up if she was just over at a friend's house. There'd be a phone call."

O'Malley took another long thoughtful drag on his cigarette and blew the smoke out with an exaggerated *phhhhhhh* sound. "Yeah, what else can we do? Tears me up. Always has. You never get used to it."

"O'Malley, damn it, how many time have I told you there's no smoking in here. This is the friggin' police station. Put that damn thing out."

"Fuck you. You're the chief of police here. You make the rules."

"Well, at least stop flicking your ashes in my goddamn coffee cup. I wasn't finished with that." He snatched the cup just as O'Malley was flicking another ash. "Oh look, now you're flickin' your ashes on my desk. You're gonna burn the place down."

"Yeah, because some perp stole my coffee-cup ashtray."

"Look, Patrick, c'mon, I know what these bastards do, and why do they do it. And it's not pretty."

"No, it's not." O'Malley leaned back, hooked his thumbs in his belt, and stretched his legs further out in front of him. He was wearing cowboy boots.

Corsetti was pacing back and forth.

"Some of these creeps don't kill their victims immediately. Some of them, well, they make like on-the-spot adoptions. They steal the kid and keep her alive."

"Yeah, I've heard of that." Corsetti nods his head. "Poor kid sometimes turns up somewhere years and years later."

"Jimmy, you know exactly what we're talking about here. We're talking about sick people who abuse and torture kids. And kill 'em. That's a fact."

O'Malley got up and crushed his cigarette on one of Corsetti's paperweights.

"You know something, O'Malley? That's a fuckin' nasty habit."

"What? Me enjoying a little smoke? Well, you wanna know something, pal, stealing coffee cups, that's an even nastier habit."

"Aw, shit." Corsetti threw up his hands and paced around the room. "So what we're saying is that we got a pedophile here?"

"Yes."

Corsetti got a clean cup and poured himself another coffee.

"And they kill to cover up their crime."

"Or hide the poor kid in their basement for years. Pray God she's just missing. Yeah, yeah, I know, *looks* like abduction, and child abductions often end in … God almighty. We have jobs to do." Corsetti put the coffee cup down and wiped his face with the palms of his hands.

"Come on, O'Malley. All this bullshit is getting us nowhere."

"Nowhere? Yeah, it's just the idle speculations of two cops trying to solve the mystery of a little girl's disappearance. She's vanished into thin air; how do you find thin air?"

"That's why you're here for Christ's sake. To help me figure this thing out. To tell us what to do. And all you do is come up with gruesome generalizations that may or may not have much to do with finding Constance Carmichael. She could be alive, held somewhere by some sadistic asshole. Maybe right here in this village. Well, where do we start; c'mon, O'Malley, where do we start."

"You know where to start. You've already started. You start with all the routine things. Interview all the usual suspects. Look in all the likely places. But, remember, if some guy just waltzed into the village and abducted Constance and no one saw anything suspicious, then, pal, we really have our work cut out for us."

"Then let's cut the bad-guy seminar and get to work, " said Corsetti.

O'Malley was sitting on the radiator. He got up and walked over to Corzetti. "We *are* working. First, let's think about some local guy, a respectable citizen who leads a secret pedophilic life. A respectable citizen who for years has fought off the desire to molest a child then one day he sees Constance and snaps; she's his flavor, and he gives in to the impulse. The dam breaks." O'Malley thumps his fists into his chest.

"Think this is the first time he's struck?" asked Corsetti.

"Well, *here* anyway," said O'Malley. "So we got no pattern."

"Yeah, so I'm guessing that this is probably some guy passing through town," said Corsetti."

This thought of it being a stranger somehow seems satisfying, even reassuring to Corsetti.

O'Malley walked over to the window and sat on the radiator again. "OK, some stranger enticed her into his car. You know, the old 'help me find my dog' routine." O'Malley's pacing back and forth. Corsetti is following him with his eyes as if he's watching the ball in a tennis match.

"Yeah, you like to think he's a stranger and not some respectable local guy: not a teacher, priest, or the janitor at the elementary school, " said O'Malley.

"Priest! Priest! For Christ's sake, O'Malley, stop that. Come down to earth. Leave priests out of this."

"OK, don't blow a gasket" and under his breath, turning away, O'Malley looks at the ceiling and says, "fucking altar boy."

"C'mon," said Corsetti. "I know we've got to suspect everybody. That's the key. Yeah, yeah, yeah, OK, maybe even a priest. We know child abusers are often members of the family, the extended family. But we're not looking for an abuser here. We're looking for an abductor. "

"You're right. And that's an entirely different thing. Family members—uncles, grandfathers, yeah, even priests—they don't abduct and kill, they molest and abuse. They depend on the child's fear to keep their crime a secret. There's no need to hide the crime with murder." O'Malley was standing in the middle of the room, hands on his hips.

"Hey, teachers," said Corsetti. "They have all kinds of opportunities. Constance went to the elementary school. She also went to that ballet school up on Glengary Road."

"Obviously." O'Malley turns to Corsetti with his arms outstretched, palms turned up. "I read that in the report, too. "You think there's a connection at the elementary school, the teachers there? You know, I'm not much worried about the ballet school," said O'Malley. "People don't often disappear from ballet schools. The instructress doesn't go around molesting and killing her students. That would be bad for business."

"Yeah, but what about some bastard lurking around the ballet school watching all the little girls? C'mon, O'Malley. Why not?"

"That's possible, of course."

"But, come on, Patrick, do you mean that in the whole history of crime there's never been a ballet school murder or disappearance? Well, pal, that might be exactly what we've got here."

"Look, Jimmy, of course, there have been ballet-school-related crimes. But there are hundreds of swishy little ballet schools in New York City, and never in all my years have I heard of a ballet school crime. So what I mean is this, on the likelihood scale, a ballet school for little girls in a little suburban village is not where I'd start looking for an evil child-molesting monster. But don't get me wrong, I'm not counting it out; I'm not letting any of those people off the hook. I'm just saying it's unlikely, that's all."

"OK," said Corsetti, "there's a start. Hey, there's Mrs. Petrovsky's son. You know him, don't you? You've seen him. Drives around in that blue Jaguar. Name's Vladimir. How about him for a top creep candidate?"

"There are plenty of fancy foreign cars in this town. Never noticed his. From what I've heard, he's a pretty typical harmless little mamma's boy. But, hey, know what, some mamma's boys have been notorious serial killers."

"Now we're cooking. He plays with those little girls all the time. Takes them all over the place in that fancy car."

"Yeah, right," said O'Malley, "I've heard that, but I also know that's his job. But I'll concede you this, pal, he is an interesting suspect. Maybe even a likely one … if not an obvious one. Maybe too obvious. So you're right, there might be a ballet school connection. Maybe that's where someone, *our someone*, first saw Constance. Maybe at a recital. So look, no problem, we'll definitely talk to Vladimir, his mother, and everyone else associated with the school. OK but right now let's think about some less obvious people."

"Then you're agreeing that weird Vladimir is a, what's the term, person of interest?"

"Didn't I say that? Twice. Want me to say it again? We'll get around to him. And to his mother."

O'Malley got up from his perch on the radiator. "We'll talk to everyone who knew Constance. Go everywhere Constance went. Yes, even to that damn ballet school on the hill."

"Not such a big deal, right? This is a small village for Christ's sake; it's not New York City. It's a village," said Corsetti.

"Yeah that does make it a little easier, I suppose. But not only do we have to talk to people, we have to go to all the likely places and look around. Do routine police work. Gumshoeing. Remember, this may be a little village but it's got a big garbage dump and a really, really big river."

"Oh, shit. Damn." Corsetti's right hand flew to his chin. "Oh, my God, I hadn't even thought about the dump. Or the river. Good God, imagine that fucking dump. Shit, we'll have to sift through that dump."

"Right. Then there's the river, the whole damn Hudson River and the Croton River below the dam." O'Malley extended both his arms like wings.

"Oh, my God, the dam, the river, the reservoir, the dump, the woods. Jesus, all of a sudden our little village is huge."

O'Malley lit another cigarette. "That's what's so tough. These bastards hide the bodies. What's worse, what makes this kind of crime worse is that they are essentially *motiveless* crimes—perpetrated against a random victim."

"Don't keep telling me what's so tough about it," said Corsetti. "Tell me how we're gonna solve it. How are we gonna find Constance? How we gonna find this, ah, killer? Hey, wait a minute. 'Motiveless?' What do you mean 'motiveless?' You said the motive was sexual; you said it was pedophilia."

"That's not the motive, that's the disease. It's possible there is no connection whatsoever between the perp and Constance. At least no clear, ordinary connection. And if that's true, then this is not your ordinary run-of-the-mill crime in the sense that there's no *regular* motive like robbery or jealousy or hate or revenge. The kind of thing that happens among people who know each other, are married, or related, or in business together. If someone in this village didn't abduct Constance with a premeditated plan and only one person is involved and he's a complete stranger at that, then right off the bat there's no web of evidence. It's an impulsive crime. We've got no beneficiaries to trace, no insurance policies, no stolen jewels, no loot, no payroll, and no leads. Essentially from that standpoint, a motiveless crime. Just a child. Just one child. Vanished. Gone." O'Malley straightened up, shrugged and held his hands out palms up.

"What we need is a witness. Someone who saw something on Thursday around the time she disappeared. Wonder if this guy has done this before?" Corsetti asked. "And will he do it again? Don't these guys get caught because they do it more than once?" Through this entire confab Corsetti had been taking notes. Making lists of where they had to go and what they had to do. Making lists of the people and the organizations he'd have to contact.

"Yeah, of course, that happens," answered O'Malley. "We can check that angle in the local communities and even in New York. But neither one of us can remember that it's ever happened here or even nearby. Nowhere around here, far as either one of us knows."

"So what do we do, Pat, wait for it to happen again? Wait for a pattern to develop? "

"Yeah, sure, right, it's true. Lots of times these guys *are* serial killers. That's why investigating the first one is tough."

"But, c'mon, O'Malley, how do we know this is the first one? *His* first one? This guy could have abducted and killed a whole passel of little girls. All over the country. We're only looking at one local disappearance. He could be good at covering up his tracks. Maybe no bodies have ever been found. That's the best cover-up of them all, to dispose of the body so it can never be found. "

"We don't know whether this is the first one. True. But once we check and find no record of recent disappearances—and, again, that's relatively easy to check—we're left with no pattern and with the assumption that this might be the guy's first."

"Circles, circles, we're going round in circles." Corsetti was getting impatient. He wanted to get on with it, to stop this speculation. Get out into the street, interview neighbors, everybody. Cut out this damn seminar.

But O'Malley wanted to continue his exploration of the criminal mind. He couldn't stop. Not right at this moment. He went on ... "This guy's a killer because he knows that molesting little girls is a crime. A damn serious one. That's why he destroys the evidence. Child rapists are not popular even in prison. He knows all this. He knows right from wrong. He's not insane. They often wish they weren't that way. At least down deep. They hate themselves for being so weak. For giving in to impulse. But do it once, and they'll have to do it again. It gets addictive. "

"Yes, and damn it, Patrick, I now know as well as you that for all our speculation even when and if we find Constance, we may not be any closer to finding her abductor."

The language of the dance [of the bees sends] them out to search for flowers of a certain perfume ... . [and when found they] whirl for one second in the hostile madness of love. ... and their magnificent eyes, mirrors once of the exuberant flowers, flashing back the blue light in the innocent pride of summer, now, softened by suffering, reflect only the anguish and distress of their end.

— From, *The Life of the Bee*
by Maurice Maeterlinck

O'Malley walked up the steps and across the porch to the front door of the Petrovsky School of Classical Ballet. He wore his dark blue suit, black tie, and black wing tips—the outfit he wears to funerals.

"Jeez," he thought, "they sure spruced this place up. Shows you what a little money can do."

Ignoring the bell, he knocked with his knuckles on the door's beveled etched glass. He had never really seen Mrs. Petrovsky up close; she wasn't one to walk around town. Stayed pretty much to herself. But he did remember someone saying that she was one sweet looking lady. "Maybe she'll come to the door and be in one of those tight, black leotards," he thought.

It was late afternoon. Mrs. Spertano was in the kitchen preparing a Waldorf salad for the Petrovsky's early supper. She'd leave it in the refrigerator. When O'Malley knocked the second time, she wiped her hands on her white apron and went to the front door.

"Why it's Mr. O'Malley. Hello, Patrick," she said. "Come to talk with the Petrovsky's about Constance?"

"That's right."

"She's over at Mrs. Fletcher's. But Vladimir is upstairs. Do you want to talk to him?"

"Yes."

"I'll get him."

O'Malley stood in the vestibule. He noticed that a pile of unopened mail was stacked on the settee along with the latest issue of *Vogue*, thick as a phonebook. Then he began to look at the pictures of Mrs. Petrovsky lining the walls of the hallway. "Mmm mmm, she sure looks good in her underwear," he was looking at the *New York Times Sunday* magazine picture of Mrs. Petrovsky performing in the *Seven Deadly Sins*.

Vladimir came down the stairs and walked up behind O'Malley.

"You wanted to talk to me?"

O'Malley turned and smiled. "Look at this guy," he thought," What a piece of work."

"Yes, I do, Mr. Petrovsky."

Vladimir, as usual, was dressed in his white shirt and black pants. He looked like a priest without his collar. He had no flower in his buttonhole. He didn't feel this day called for such light touches.

"I want to talk to you about one of your ballet students, Constance Carmichael. She's disappeared you know." O'Malley watched Vladimir's face carefully.

"Of course, I know." He lowered his head. "Let's go into the parlor." Vladimir led the way. "Sit here," he said motioning to a chair. "Now, let's see, you're—?"

"Patrick Joseph O'Malley, lad, NYPD retired. Detective." He didn't offer his hand to Vladimir. He just unbuttoned his suit coat and sat down on the maroon velvet Chippendale wing chair that Vladimir had motioned him to. Although O'Malley had conducted hundreds of such interviews, he now felt a twinge of discomfort in the embrace of the chair's wings, which stuck out like giant horse blinders on either side of his head. He leaned forward moving his butt onto the edge of the chair. Vladimir pulled the straight-back chair out from under the desk, a Jacobian roll top, an impressive antique made of gleaming mahogany veneer with satinwood inlays.

"Nice place you've got here. All spit and polish and antiques. Neat and clean as a pin. Looks like an old English manor house. Hey, Vladimir, ever been down there to the Biltmore Estate. Down in North Carolina. Asheville, North Carolina. In the mountains. You should. I have. You'd like it. It'd knock your sock off." O'Malley shifted forward in the chair and swiveled his head around the room.

"No, I haven't." Vladimir settled himself in his chair and crossed his hands on his lap.

"All this stuff English? Are you English, of English descent?" Of course O'Malley knew better but now more at ease, he thought he'd indulge himself with a little humor.

"No. We are Russian. Some of this furniture is English. A lot is French."

"Russian. That right? You were *born* in Russia?"

"No. My mother was and my grandparents. So, Mr. O'Malley, you're here to talk about Constance Carmichael. The disappearance of Constance Carmichael."

"That's right. You knew her, of course." That was a slip. O'Malley had not meant to use the past tense.

"Of course I do."

"Vladimir, when was the last time you saw Constance, the last time she was here?"

"I think it was Wednesday, for her lesson. I could check the schedule."

"Yes, I'd like to look at the schedule before I leave."

"Yes. You may."

"Vladimir, what was your relationship with Constance?"

"Relationship? I had none. She was a student here. She *is* a student here."

"Well, what is your relationship with the students? I mean, how do you interact with them?"

"I simply help Mrs. Petrovsky run the school. I keep the schedule, for example. Things like that."

"You talk with the girls, don't you?"

"Why, yes, of course I do."

"And they talk with you?"

"Yes, of course. Some small talk. But there's not much time for talk. They are here for their lessons. They come and go."

"Don't you sometimes take them to the park for picnics?"

"Yes, on occasion I do."

"Special occasions?"

"No. Not really. Just sometimes on pretty days."

"Weekdays or weekends?"

"Usually weekdays, but both."

"Was that part of the school's scheduled activities?"

"No, not really. I just did that. I liked the girls and they liked to ride in the car and go to the park."

"Did Constance ever go with you to the park, with the other girls?"

"Yes."

"Did you have any kind of special relationship with Constance?"

"No. She was just one of the ballerinas, and we tried to make them all feel welcome here. You might say that our outings were like any school's extracurricular activities."

"When you saw Constance on Wednesday, did you notice anything different about her, her mood, for example?"

"No. We didn't talk as I recall. She came for her lesson and went home."

"How often did she come here? Did she come every Wednesday for a lesson?"

"No, the scheduling is flexible, as much as possible to accommodate the children's other activities. They would come two or maybe three times a week. Never on Thursday. The school is closed on Thursdays"

"Who brought Constance to her lessons?"

"Her mother, Mrs. Carmichael."

"Do you recall anyone else ever bringing her here?"

"No."

"Did she ever come alone?"

"Sometimes, but very seldom. Some of the older students might come alone. But not many and not often. Very seldom. As I think about it, almost never."

"Well, let me ask you this, Vladimir. Did you ever see anyone, I mean *anyone* hanging around the park when you were there with the girls? With Constance?" O'Malley relaxed, crossed his legs, and sat back in the chair's velvet embrace. He wanted his body language to convey complete casualness.

"No. I was never really looking for anyone. There were always, I guess, a few other people in the park, mostly fishermen, one or two, on the breakwater. That's all." Vladimir crossed his hands and interlocked his fingers, tenting them in his lap.

"Were you ever aware that one of the fishermen noticed you and the girls?

"Oh, I am sure they were aware of us, but in my recollections they didn't pay much attention. They were smoking cigarettes, talking among themselves, or concentrating on their floats."

"Did you ever walk with the girls on the breakwater?"

"Yes, when we were there, we would go down to the breakwater."

"Well, wouldn't that put you close to the fisherman, close enough for a wave, a holler, a hello?"

"No. As a matter of fact we were always pretty far away from them. Down toward the other end of the breakwater. They seemed to favor the south end. We would generally go down opposite the picnic tables at the north end."

"Lately, around here, did you notice any strange cars, I mean cars you maybe didn't recognize, parked here on Glengary Road near the school?

You know up the street or out front?" O'Malley bent forward, then, thinking that his body language might be threatening, leaned back in the chair and crossed his legs.

"No. I don't think I ever noticed one. Don't recall any." Now Vladimir crossed his legs. O'Malley admired those English calfskin buckle shoes. He couldn't help making a remark about them. So he leaned forward and said, "Hey, nice kickers. Now I'd bet those are English shoes. Am I right?"

"Yes, Vladimir smiled, they are. From a place in Northhampton, Crockett & Jones."

"Real fancy. They sure look comfortable. I have a pair of old cowboy boots. They're comfortable, too. Well, you know people always say how comfortable cowboy boots are, but you know, that's not quite true. Walking up on the heels takes getting used to. Other people don't think they can be comfortable 'cause of the pointy toes, but generally they are. Least when they're broken in good." O'Malley leaned back in the chair, raised his hands, and cupped them to the back of his head. Then he uncupped them, put his palms on his knees, and leaned forward.

"Vladimir, did Constance ever tell you about anyone—a teacher, a family friend, anyone—she, well, let's say feared? Did she ever talk to you about anything like that?" O'Malley noticed no perceptible change in Vladimir's relaxed facial expression.

"'Feared'? What do you mean by that?"

"Well, I mean what I said. I mean did she ever confide in you? Tell you anything personal about her life, her friends, her parents?"

"No. We went on picnics, always with the other girls, told stories, and sang songs. She had no reason to fear anyone. And no reason to confide in me. She is a little girl, Mr. O'Malley, we didn't 'confide.'" Vladimir spoke the words matter of factly.

"Well, did she ever seem ... sort of withdrawn, sort of sad?" For effect O'Malley paused between the words "seem" and "sort of."

"Sad? No. She was a happy little girl. Not complicated or moody. But then I didn't really spend that much time with her." Vladimir was still sitting upright, rather stiffly in the chair with his fingers laced together resting in his lap, motionless.

"Well," O'Malley spread his arms out toward Vladimir with his palms turned up as he had done in Corsetti's office, "no mood changes you noticed?"

Vladimir did not pause for even a microsecond and answered in a calm even voice, "No. Really. Never. When we were together it was most often with the other little girls; those were, well, just happy playful times."

"I know that Vladimir, but you must try to help us. Can you think of anything that might help us find her?"

"I am trying to help you, Mr. O'Malley. But this is hard. I cannot imagine this has happened. I cannot understand why this has happened. All those girls are so innocent and happy. That's why it was fun to be around them. Will you ever find Constance?" Vladimir stood up and put his hands into his pockets as he spoke.

"Well, Vladimir, I assure you will do everything possible to find her … and to find her safe."

"Will she be dead?" Vladimir stared down at the floor.

"Truthfully, Vladimir, I don't know. I just don't know." O'Malley got up slowly.

"Oh, the schedule. You wanted to see the schedule," said Vladimir.

After O'Malley left, Vladimir walked slowly down the hallway running his fingers across the surface of the pictures like a boy running a stick down a picket fence. He went through the kitchen into the sunroom. He looked through the window into the garden. He had tears in his eyes, and he felt them trickle down his cheeks.

That night Vladimir ate no dinner. He just sat on the big leather sofa in his suite with two pillows on his lap. At around 9 o'clock he went to his side of the bathroom. He flicked the light on and approached the sink. Something caught his eye, a black spot in the sink. It was a spider and surprised by the sudden light, it started to scale the slopping walls of the sink. Vladimir winced, "God, how ugly you are." he thought. Slowly, without taking his eyes off the spider, he reached up and pulled a tissue from the chrome holder above the sink. He folded it carefully lengthwise then thrust it toward the spider like a warrior thrusting his sword in the face of an advancing enemy. The spider, instantly sensing the assault, darted away.

Vladimir turned the water on. Alert to this new danger, the spider crouched, lifting his black brindled belly off the surface of the sink and worked his mandibles back and forth. The miniature tsunami moved quickly toward him and he skittered up and away from it. Vladimir pushed him back with his tissue sword and gave the faucet another turn. The water caught the spider, enveloped him and washed him down the drain. The slime on the sides of the pipe was to the spider like glue. It held him and he held it as the water washed over his furry back. Vladimir turned the water off. The spider was still crouching in the slime as Vladimir brushed his teeth, washed his face and hands, flicked the light off and left the bathroom.

During the hours he lay awake in bed, he found himself wishing that he could as easily wash away his sadness and loneliness as he had the black spider, as easily wash away the evil impulses that he had discovered in his own heart.

After an hour or two, the spider climbed tentatively up and over the lip of the drain and crawled out into the now dry sink bowl, into the now dark room. His eyes, mounted on flexible stalks, rotated searching the darkness. He shivered to flick the dampness off his fluffy back and moved forward stiffly with bestial caution as if on stilts and then lowered his belly to the surface of the sink and glided slowly up its side. His mandibles were set in an expression of wry satisfaction. He had eluded the towering predator. And the water. He paused on the edge of the sink and looked down. Then slipped over its side, floating to the tile floor below like an ash descending from a fire. He loved the darkness. He was its brother. This was his time, his place.

The fairest things have fleetest end,
Their scent survives their close;
But the rose's scent is bitterness
To him that loved the rose.
— From *Daisy* by Francis Thompson

A week or so after interviewing Vladimir, O'Malley returned to the school to talk with Mrs. Patterson, the piano player. "I hardly knew the girls, at least not by name," said Mrs. Patterson. "Never really spoke to them. The only time I looked up from the music was when Mrs. Petrovsky asked me to start, stop, or repeat a piece of music." No, she could not remember anything unusual about the particular day that Constance disappeared. The school was closed that day. Vladimir? She said that Vladimir's function was "to step and fetch it." "He is a charming, unobtrusive young man," she said, but she had never noticed anything unusual about his relationship with any of the girls.

Then came his interview with Mrs. Petrovsky herself.

During the interview, she maintained an air of queenliness. That did not particularly surprise O'Malley. Didn't most of these people try to pass themselves off as if they were related to the royal families of Imperial Russia? Had it not been for the revolution. …

She was, indeed, a truly beautiful woman, and O'Malley was certainly not immune to the power such beauty bestows upon such a woman. She wore her regal raiment with a nonchalant and natural hauteur that would have disarmed even the most cynical, hardened interrogator. In other words, in spite of all his years' of experience, O'Malley felt a bit off—not at the top of his game. So the interview was stiff, formal and apparently unproductive.

"I understand that the school is closed on Thursdays. Every Thursday?"

"That is true."

"What do you do on your free weekday, on Thursdays?"

"Any number of things. Mostly I visit Mrs. Fletcher."

"She's a friend of yours?"

"Yes, you might say that, a friend who happens to have an absolutely lovely indoor pool.

"You go there to take a swim?"

"Yes, for the exercise. We do a series of water exercises designed by a ballerina for ballerinas."

O'Malley's imagination instantly displayed a tableau—Mrs. Petrovsky gliding through the sapphire water in a pink skin-tight one-piece bathing suit. A lovely albeit distracting vision.

"What time do you go there? Do you have a regular time?"

"Well, yes and no. It varies according to our whims. So sometimes in the morning, sometimes in the afternoon."

"How do you get there?

"Sometimes Vladimir drives me. Other times I take the car myself."

"On the Thursday that Constance disappeared do you remember if you went to see Mrs. Fletcher in the morning or the afternoon."

"No, I do not."

"Do you realize, Mrs. Petrovsky, had you gone in the afternoon on that day, late afternoon, you might have seen Constance at or near the drugstore? Can you remember if you might have seen her, seen a car, seen anyone near the drugstore, anything like that?"

"Mr. O'Malley, it is impossible for me to remember any particulars of that day. Perhaps I did not even go to see Mrs. Fletcher that day. Perhaps I stayed home, lounged around, took a long, hot bath, read a book." she smiled a delicious smile that could almost be taken for a subtle tease.

O'Malley's imagination threw up another distracting image.

Mrs. Petrovsky thought of O'Malley—who lived down by the river in a part of the village she had never seen—as a rather odious commoner trespassing on her nobility. Although, she thought, he was unexpectedly handsome even in his rumpled dark blue suit. She didn't think much of New York City policemen. In her experience, they were rude, tough talking, rather low-class, uneducated, authoritarian men, and worse, most often Irishmen. She had never met an NYPD detective, but suspected they were of the same ilk. In spite of the fact that he was somewhat well spoken and "unexpectedly handsome," she didn't see anything in his manner to change her opinions.

Things are never what they seem. Skim milk masquerades as cream.

> — From *H.M.S. Pinafore*
> by Sir William Schwenck Gilbert

O'Malley was if anything a thoughtful man and, as we have already established, a voracious reader. In addition to the bestsellers, he read everything he could get his hands on. Where he picked up this habit, no one knew.

While most of us think in sentences, O'Malley thought in paragraphs. Indeed, he spoke in paragraphs. What most men could say in a word, O'Malley would take a hundred words. He was never at a loss for words. He could talk your ear off. To him nothing was simple. He had to look at everything from every angle. Bottom side up and top side down. The man was a walking dictionary. One of his favorite subjects was evil. "Oh, for the love of God," said his pal Corsetti, "don't ever get him started on that unless you've got two day's worth of beer, breakfast, lunch, and dinner."

Twenty years or more of police work in Manhattan—on the Upper East Side—had taught O'Malley a lot about the subject of evil. One thing he knew was that often, when evil stands before us, we cannot see it. It is so ordinary as to be invisible. That's because good and evil meld together like oil paints on an artist's brush.

He had read Hannah Arendt's book, *Eichmann in Jerusalem: A Report on the Banality of Evil.* That phrase "the banality of evil" stuck in his head. He thought that it was not just the people but also the perpetrator himself who becomes habituated to the view that his crime is not evil but just the way things are.

It would, of course, be so much easier for us to navigate between heaven and hell if evil were in fact *always* ugly, never banal. Easier for us if evil people and evil places were instantly recognizable simply because of their ugliness. We are conditioned from childhood to associate the bright and the beautiful, the normal, the regular, the ordinary with good and all the opposite with evil. We become conditioned to believe that beautiful people, surely they cannot be evil.

O'Malley knew from long experience that there are monsters in our midst masquerading as ordinary, if not beautiful, people. Husbands, wives, brothers, friends. In-laws. Wolves as lambs. Violence as docility.

That's why once a crime is solved, there is so often what O'Malley called the "Aha Factor." Once the tangles are untangled and the pattern clear, it seems that we somehow knew all along what the solution was. No. Not in any conscious sense. But subliminally. It never fails, after the monster is caught they ask his elementary school teacher what sort of boy he was. The teacher has been there twenty plus years, has white hair all done up in a bun, and is named something like Mrs. Abernathy. She replies, "Well, ordinary, I guess, but you know, he *was* a bit strange. Didn't have many friends. Had a funny way of looking at you." Like Mrs. Abernathy, we all know the signs in some subtle, inarticulate, "below the surface" way before the fact is revealed. After the fact, we say, "Aha, I suspected that all along. It was the way he looked at me."

Throughout his career on the streets of New York, O'Malley had those Aha moments time and time again. It taught him always to listen to the faintest whisper of his hunches. So enamored was he of the power of hunches that he'd tear examples of them out of the articles he read in the *New York Times* and underline them in the books he was reading.

(Even if they were library books!) He seldom read anything without a pencil, a notepad, and scissors nearby. He never hesitated to cut an article that interested him out of the *Times,* and his favorite one concerning hunches told of an amateur spelunker, Randy Tufts, who had a hunch there might be a never-before-discovered cavern beneath the Kartchner Ranch in Arizona. Sure enough, one day he discovered it. He kept it a secret for twelve years. When he finally told James Kartchner about the cavern beneath his ranch, the owner said, "Well, you know what, Randy, I always thought I heard this hollow sound whenever I rode my horse over that place. Never knew what to make of it. But I knew there was something there all along."

Time and again O'Malley would see parents, neighbors, friends who never heard "the hollow sounds." Or hearing them almost never would *admit* to hearing them. "What are you talking about, officer? My son? Impossible! He would never hurt a flea."

Sorry, Mrs. Dahmer. Sorry, Mrs. Manson. Sorry, Mrs. Gacy. Your once darling little boys, Jeffery, Charles, and John Wayne really are horrid monsters, and you must have known, maybe not consciously but c'mon, you knew. Mrs. Abernathy knew—why not you?

O'Malley also knew what mommies seldom know or knowing want to admit. That their precious little boys, like precious little pussycats, kill the baby bunnies they find under the lavender bush ... for the sheer fun of it. Some little boys, like all pet cats, are predators at heart. Yes, that little pet cat now sitting on mommy's lap has just licked sweet, warm blood off its paws and little claws.

O'Malley also knew something about the seductiveness of evil. He knew that, again like a pussycat, it could snuggle up soft, warm, and reassuringly to the ankles of its victims.

But, on the other hand, take Corsetti. He would not have been so sure about all this. Oh, he knew. He knew a lot. After all, he *was* a cop, too. But he knew about evil in perhaps a more academic way while O'Malley had experienced it personally. For example, O'Malley knew that there are evil priests who touch altar boys inappropriately in the sacristy and then with those same fingers lay the body of Christ on the tongues of unknowing parishioners. When confronted with the possibility of such evil, Corsetti would say, "Yes, but not Father McInerney. That's impossible. He's such a wonderful man; all the children, everybody loves him. I can't believe that," which, of course, means "I do *not want* to believe that."

It is difficult for a man to actually find and confront evil unless he first believes in its existence. To believe in evil, you must first believe in a world of spiritual forces swirling around unseen. That was the difference. O'Malley was a true believer. He believed in Satan. Corsetti, in spite of his religion, still had his doubts.

O'Malley believed in Satan because he had a hard time believing that man could be capable of such unspeakable acts on his own. He believed society needed the concept of Satan to cope with the monsters among us, to explain their gruesome actions.

By playing the Satan card, we can say, "No, these are not the acts of men. These are the acts of evil spirits that inhabit the bodies of men." That's why the frequent plea of a captured criminal is often Faustian: "The devil made me do it. Satan whispered in my ear. I did not *sell* my soul; he *stole* my soul."

O'Malley was, for example, familiar with the so-called Son of Sam killings, which had occurred in New York City. Berkowitz, who killed young women randomly, said his neighbor's dog, Sam, had told him to murder them. Indeed, Sam selected the victims. Sam was the personification of the satanic power in his life. He said he was "demon-possessed." *He* didn't do it. The devil did it through him. He was Satan's instrument.

Why Satan? Well, it's perfectly clear. Satan is forever seeking revenge on God for his banishment from Heaven. Satan is a terrorist. The only way to undermine God is to spread evil in His world. Satan recruits his terrorists from among ordinary men. He lures them into his world of darkness. There can be no other explanation. Absent Satan you are left with plain, ordinary, good persons. God does not create bad people. There could be no evil in a world created by God … unless there were a Satan. Without Satan as the instigator and engine of evil, yes, take Satan out of the equation, and you would have heaven on earth.

So it is God himself who needs Satan to account for all the evil, all the suffering in His world.

To make all this more confusing, not every evildoer, like Berkowitz, blames Satan. There are those who blame God Himself. Some say they hear the voice of *God*, not Satan, whispering in their ear. It was *God* who told me to do it, says the woman who slays her children. Why? To send them to a better place, to give them passage to the Kingdom of Heaven. She says that God told her to do it to achieve a good that transcends the apparent evilness of the act itself. Maybe that's like saying that martyrdom is not suicide.

O'Malley knew that ideas like these can lead people to flirt with evil. Leopold and Loeb, wealthy, privileged students at the University of Chicago wanted to see if they could commit the perfect crime. So one afternoon, with studied premeditation they kidnapped, murdered, and sexually mutilated a randomly selected fourteen-year-old boy. The boy, in their view, was of no great importance, certainly not in the grand scheme of things. He was a frog in a lab. After all, they were intellectuals, geniuses well above the reach, much less the sanction, of ordinary law or morality. What they did was to them merely an intellectual exercise. In reality it was a rite of passage into the world of evil. The law saw it as the crime it was, and they died for their crime.

Alfred Hitchcock's *Rope* presents a compelling dramatization based on this crime, and its bizarre motivations. O'Malley had watched the film twice.

Another example of this pathology is found in Dostoyevsky's *Crime and Punishment* where Raskolnikov, the protagonist, begins to think that if murder were really a crime, why then are Napoleon and all the other great generals who kill tens of thousands on the field of battle revered as heroes and not despised as mass murderers? Surely, he thought, measured against that metric, murdering one single worthless, despicable old woman with an ax was of no consequence whatsoever. It was simply an intellectual, moral experiment. So he did it. Why not?

These young criminals believed that they were above the law, which applies only to ordinary people. In the Neitzschean sense, Leopold and Loeb believed they were supermen. Thus, with a powerful moral alchemy, they were able to transmute their unspeakable act, to rationalize it into nothing more than what you might call an act undertaken to assert their superiority. Satan smiles.

O'Malley was up late that night sitting in his white wicker chair on the porch of his ramshackle chalet above the Croton River smoking Camels and sipping Jack Daniels. He was listening to the faint murmur of the river and the chirp of night birds, as all these thoughts of evil swam through his stream of consciousness. Although he had an open book on his lap and a pencil in his hand, he was not reading the book nor was he so much thinking about evil as he was fishing around in his mind for a way either to solve the disappearance of Constance Carmichael ... or find a way to learn to live with it.

He put the book down. "Now, let's see," he thought, "if someone were passing by Croton, what reason would he have to stop *in* Croton? You cannot just drive through Croton anymore, there's the new by-pass. There's no service station even near the exit to the village. So you wouldn't be stopping for gas. Yes, there is a little grocery store, a butcher shop, a florist. There's the Plymouth dealer. There's the gift shop down by the train station. We've checked all those places. Found nothing unusual."

He thought about how someone might drive into Croton. The four-lane by-pass looped around the village going north and south along the Hudson River. Going south it narrowed and fed into the old highway, which then turned southwest to White Plains or due south to Ossining. Heading north it went up to Peekskill and Poughkeepsie. Because of the by-pass, Croton was the only town along the river that you can't just happen to drive through. You had to exit the bypass. You had to have a reason to do that. There was little reason to stop, unless, of course, you lived in Croton or you were cruising around looking for a little girl to abduct.

"A creep like that," O'Malley continued to muse, "might be cruising the river towns. He'd come off the four-lane by-pass, loop up, and drive through town. Most likely go up there by the elementary school. He'd park, perhaps at, let's say around 2:30 in the afternoon down the street from the school and watch for a girl, a girl walking alone. If he failed there, he'd maybe drive around the streets. No one would notice. Most people would be at work. He'd see Constance. She'd stand out in her bright yellow slicker. He'd stop his car, roll down the window, ask directions, maybe directions to the dam. Yeah, he wanted to see the famous Croton dam. He'd be charming, convincing, ingratiating; he'd talk about the windy, rainy weather; 'Oh, you live just up the street … on the way to the dam? Then hop in. I'll give you a ride up the hill.' But why would Constance hop in? Could it have been someone she knew and trusted?"

Without a witness, trying to find such a person can be very difficult—often impossible. And there were no witnesses. There really are no strangers in Croton-on-Hudson because there's little reason to be a stranger in Croton. The only real points of interest are Croton Point Park, and there's nothing there except green grass, a view of the Hudson, and a few picnic tables. There's the dam. Nothing much to see there except the spillway and the reservoir. This is not a shopping center, not a tourist destination. Just a small, self-contained New York City commuter town.

All things human are subject to decay ...
— From *MacFlecknoe* by John Dryden

Vladimir was upstairs alone in his suite. He had closed the velvet curtains and was now slouched so low in that soft brandy colored couch that it looked as if he were being swallowed by it. His arms encircled and pressed a flowered brocade pillow to his chest. His eyes were closed. He was playing a game of tag with thoughts that scurried down the labyrinthine corridors of his young mind like shadows under birds.

It was as if Vladimir could only experience the present, the here and now, as if he were trapped in a narrow canal of reality cupped in the parabola of the present.

"Flowers," he thought, "were in their own way as perishable as thoughts and memories." Perhaps all the more precious for their perishability. The fresher, the more perishable. Like leftovers on the dinner table, expired flowers are nothing more than garbage. There is simply no way to pick a flower without hastening its decay and death. Even left alone unpicked, unseen in some garden or field, they wilt and die a natural death never mourned. Or, in the poet's words: "Full many a flower is born to blush unseen/And waste its sweetness on the desert air."

To Vladimir, loving flowers was like a hobby. The flowers his mother put on the bedside table in the morning would, to his practiced eye, fade if not by late afternoon, then by evening. Inevitably, they would wilt and die. If they were a longer lasting variety, like roses, he would grow tired of them anyway. He did not want to see wilted flowers, only the freshest ones. Nor did he want to see stale, cloudy water in the vase, so a ceaseless procession of flowers—from the garden in spring and summer and from the florist in the winter—would be martyred every morning to satisfy his passion. And then, some at the zenith of their beauty, thrown away, discarded as the refuse of his peculiar passion for them and the pleasure he took in them.

There was, of course, nothing wrong with sacrificing flowers. Flowers were made by a thoughtful and benevolent God to serve the pleasure of man. To use them for pleasure and to take pleasure in them is part of the divine plan. Not to do so, now that would be wrong.

Whether it was wrong to use other things, little girls for example, solely for pleasure, well that was another matter. He adored both flowers and little girls. They were so much alike. What did that make him? Why nothing more than a little bit eccentric. There was, therefore, no moral equation to be solved. If there were a hierarchy among living things, he was disinclined to accept it. Like the flowers taken out with yesterday's trash, he could hardly remember all the little girls he had known. There were always other little girls to take the place of all the forgotten ones. If there had been something special about her—what was her name, Constance?—he had forgotten what it was. Now it was Ellen.

24

They were possessed with such a Rage or,
To give it it's proper Name, such an Itching for their Flowers,
As to give often three thousand Crowns for a
Tulip that pleased their Fancies;
A Disease that ruined several rich Families.
— From *Travels Through Holland, 1743,*
by Monsieur de Blainville

O'Malley had, in his own words, "gumshoed his way through town." He had questioned Joe Rosone, manager of the Plymouth dealership, and learned that no stranger had stopped in to inquire about a car or anything else that fateful Thursday. Same thing at the gift shop. The grocer. The butcher. The florist. Same thing at Carnaby's. Nothing unusual seems to have happened in Croton-on-Hudson on the Thursday Constance Carmichael disappeared. Absolutely nothing.

They did the best they could with the dump. Dozens of volunteers clothed in HAZMAT suits had crossed and re-crossed the mini mountains of refuse an arm's length apart. The authorities had set up grids and run front loaders into each grid one after the other to turn over and sift the trash. They found nothing. Not even the cadaver dogs turned up anything.

They dragged the Hudson close to the western shoreline from Senasqua Park to Tellers Point. They drained the duck pond. They searched Croton Point Park and parks in surrounding communities north and south— Dobbs Park, Black Rock Park, Silverdale, Paradise Island County Park, even the Brinton Brook Bird Sanctuary and Arboretum on the northern boundary of the village. The cemetery. They used the dogs. They searched the little park below the dam and the entire length of the Croton River from below the dam to where it empties into the Hudson at Croton Bridge. A posse of men searched the woods surrounding the Croton reservoir on foot and on horseback and with dogs while others took boats around its entire shoreline. They dragged close to shore with those awful grappling hooks. Nothing.

The police departments in the surrounding towns had turned up nothing either. The state police had turned up nothing. O'Malley had personally questioned everyone who lived up and down the street from the Carmichael's home. He talked to kids, parents, the janitors, and the teachers at the elementary school, not just those who had had Constance in their classes. Everyone. Yes, he even questioned the priest at the Catholic Church.

They had done everything they could do. There was nothing left to do but wait.

"God has covered your bones with flesh. Your flesh is soft and warm. In your flesh there is blood. God has put skin outside and it covers your flesh and blood like a coat . . . . How kind of God to give you a body! I hope your body will not get hurt.

"How easy it would be to hurt your poor little body!

" . . . If a great knife were run through your body, the blood would come out. If a great box were to fall on your head, your head would be crushed. If you were to fall out a window, your neck would be broken. If you were not to eat some food for a few days, your little body would be very sick, your breath would stop, and you would grow cold, and you would soon be dead."

— From *The Peep of Day: A Series of the Earliest Religious Instruction the Infant Mind Is Capable of Receiving, with Verses Illustrative of the Subjects*
by Mrs. Favell Lee Bevan Mortimer

The horrible thing about a death or a disappearance like this is that for those on the periphery very little if anything really changes. After the initial shock, grief, and fear, life for them goes on. Normal activities, if they paused at all, quickly resume their regular pace.

This was true even at Mrs. Petrovsky's School of Classical Ballet. In fact its popularity, was apparently unaffected by the mystery surrounding the disappearance of one of its students. The mothers of aspiring ballerinas realized almost immediately that the disappearance of the Carmichael girl had left a vacancy at the school, and soon after a discreet passage of time the Petrovsky calendar filled up with audition appointments.

Among the girls who most impressed Mrs. Petrovsky was Ellen Sheffield, a lithe, unusually tall nine-year-old child with a sparkling smile. It was she who was chosen to fill the single empty slot in the school's roster of students. Mrs. Sheffield was overjoyed. "Life works in strange ways," she thought. Thus, what was a tragedy of immeasurable proportions for the Carmichaels became a significant opportunity for the Sheffields.

Ellen Sheffield was a natural flirt. She could do these tiny things with her eyes, things too subtle to describe. Things too subtle for a language of words. She had apparently come into the world equipped with a paralinguistic vocabulary of truly amazing proportions. Every time she moved, if she wanted to, she could send a message designed to titillate and tease. Or to help her get her own sweet way. She was, in fact, a master in the art of getting her own sweet way. Having charmed Mrs. Petrovsky almost immediately, she set her sights on Vladimir, and the two of them quickly fell into the habit of speaking this secret body language at every possible moment. Soon it led to the language of touch. Oh, nothing that rose to the level of molestation. And Vladimir and Ellen grew to relish their excitingly delicious game.

Whenever the opportunity arose, albeit there were few, they would set out together to explore every continent in this world of titillation and tease. They crossed boundaries in a kind of playful innocence. Each savored feelings they had never felt before, never even imagined. It was, for them, a feast set at the table of seduction. Innocent foreplay, the kind that has no expectation of climax, closure, or conclusion.

Vladimir, for example, would touch her tenderly on her shoulder or behind her neck under her hair, not so much with sexual intimacy as with wonder and adoration, as one might softly touch the petals of an exotic orchid, exploring the geography of beauty, innocence, and immaturity. For her part, she was not so much flirting with Vladimir as she was flirting with—experimenting with—the power of her own awakening femininity and sexuality. She was exploring the emerging promise and power of her womanhood. Sometimes beckoning to it, teasing it out of herself. Come out! Come out! I know you're in there. Come out. Let's play.

For Vladimir, full-blown womanhood was somehow harsh if not coarse. Surrounded as he was by a world of prepubescent girls, he found maturity in women undesirable. But the fresh, innocent hint of it in Ellen was both mystifying and exciting: the perfume of her innocence juxtaposed with the more worldly scent of her potential womanhood. The hint of the tiger in the tiger cub. So they played their game in the hallways and the dressing rooms and upstairs in his children's paradise. There were no scolding parents to sour their stolen moments of play. During intermissions in their game, he would watch her stretch at the barre, filling himself with the radiant sight of her.

Vladimir and Ellen were like lovers so obsessed with one another that they were not conscious of those around them, like the lovers one sees in a trance of passion in a restaurant or a train station unaware of the crowds around them. For the most part, although they had grown somewhat careless, they were unobserved. The other ballerinas, unlike Ellen, were too unsophisticated or too preoccupied with their lessons to notice anything remarkable in the behavior of these two toward one another. Besides, Vladimir, whenever in the company of the other ballerinas, showed no open signs of favoritism. So, it was not the dancers who recognized the choreography of their flirtatious dance, it was Mrs. Petrovsky. "Good God," she thought, "no sooner does Constance disappear from the stage than like a fickle Balanchine, Vladimir chooses yet another little flower to lavish his favors upon."

Mrs. Petrovsky took his infatuations much more seriously than he. To him, trapped in the surroundings of the ballet school, it was nothing more than a diversion, one, of course, not without its own special dangers. Mrs. Petrovsky found the game more serious, dangerous not because she was worried about its moral implications, that never occurred to her, but because their game took the spotlight away from her.

So what for Vladimir was little more than a game to pass the time was for Mrs. Petrovsky a bitter challenge to her supremacy. But because Mrs. Petrovsky said nothing to him or changed her behavior toward him, Vladimir was unaware of this. After all he was knee-deep in very pretty little girls, and they were, to him, the most congenial and convenient of playthings. A circumstance of his environment. After all, his mother saw to that. She recruited them. Given the nature of his life, they were the only thing that satisfied his need for companionship, the only chance he had for novelty, stimulation, and diversion. For Mrs. Petrovsky, however, they, his favorites, had become what she perceived as a threat to her sovereignty over the love of her son. She was, after all, and meant to remain forever, the Queen Bee.

Time, like an ever-rolling stream
Bears all its sons away.

— From an old tune quoted in
Iron John by Robert Bly

Six months after the disappearance of Constance, her coffee-stained file folder was still on Corsetti's desk, but all the normal rhythms of village life had returned. Commuters came and went. Caddis flies, stoneflies, mayflies, and their kin were dimpling and dancing across the surface of the Croton River. Sparrows in the early morning and bats in the evening feasted on them. As did the trout and blue gills.

O'Malley was standing knee deep in the waters of the Croton River. He was trying to tie a number 22 Blue Winged Olive onto the end of his leader. He had put on his reading glasses, and they now rode precariously close to the end of his nose. Still he couldn't get the leader through the eye of the hook. "Damn, now I can't even see with my reading glasses." He pushed the brim of his cap up high on his head and pushed the reading glasses up over his forehead and into his hair. Now without their aid he managed to thread the leader through the eye of the hook and tie a double cinch knot to secure it. Once that was done, he looked up and blinked to clear his eyes. They felt like they were crossed. He shook his head to realign them. That's when he saw a bright metallic flash in the woods. "What the hell's that?" He squinted, trying to focus through the trees.

It was a car. A dark blue Jaguar. It was parked under the trees next to his light blue Chevy Impala station wagon at the end of the dirt road that led off the main road and ended in a grassless turnaround overlooking the riverbank. He blinked when he saw Vladimir Petrovsky sitting on the top of the Jaguar with his legs dangling down through the open sunroof. Vladimir's arms were spread out slanting behind him like the legs of a tripod with his palms resting on the top of the car. He wore his usual white shirt and black pants.

He was watching O'Malley. O'Malley was watching him.

"What th' hell is that Petrovsky lad doing out here in the woods?" he said out loud as he reeled in his line and hooked the Blue Winged Olive in the keeper just above the reel. Without taking his eyes off Vladimir, he reversed the rod handle so the butt faced forward and the end of the rod stuck out behind him—the traditional strategy fly fishermen use to prevent jamming the tip of their long rods into the ground if they should stumble and fall. This done, he waded slowly to shore, climbed up the bank, and walked along the footpath beside the river toward the two cars.

"Mr. Petrovsky. Good day to you, sir."

"Mr. O'Malley. Good day to you, sir." Vladimir mimicked the intonations in O'Malley's greeting.

"What are you doing here? Got your feet caught in the sunroof of your fancy car?" said O'Malley smiling and looking up at Vladimir.

"I was watching you. Watching you fish."

"Well, lad, that's not much of a show. But then the admission's free."

"And listening to the birds … and thinking." Vladimir leaned forward, raised his arms over his head, and stretched like a cat awakening from a nap.

"Thinking? What about?" O'Malley walked closer to the car.

"Oh, everything and nothing. I don't know. Things."

"Have you got a lot of things to think about?"

"Maybe. Then again, I suppose, no, I don't." Vladimir shrugged his shoulders.

O'Malley placed the butt of his slender bamboo rod on the ground beside him and leaned the rod carefully against the side of the Jaguar. Then he leaned belly-first against its front fender. He took a pack of Camels out of his fishing vest, reached up and pushed the brim back on his NY Yankees baseball cap. He struck a match, cupped his hands, bent to put his elbows on the hood, and lit the cigarette. He was facing the river, and without looking up he raised his hand with the cigarettes and said, "Vladimir, want a smoke?"

"I have my own, Mr. O'Malley."

"Good. I don't like to smoke alone. And, listen, lad, if we're gonna have a smoke together, you've got to cut the formal stuff. You've got to call me either Pat, Patrick, O'Malley, or P.J., take your pick."

"What are you fishing for P.J.?" Vladimir reached into his shirt pocket and pulled out a filtered Tareyton. Then he took a silver Ronson lighter out of his pant's pocket, cupped his hands around the lighter, and lit the cigarette.

"Trout," said O'Malley. "Mostly brown trout and some rainbows. Some brookies in here too."

"Is the fishing good here?"

"Yeah, I'd say good. Not a lot of pressure, and they stocked upstream. Stocked some big rainbows. I know, I helped them. You can do that if you got connections." O'Malley smiled. "The rainbows, they always drop down here, into those big pools like the one out there." He pointed. "See that pool over there. The fish are there. For some reason they take only really small, itty-bitty flies this time of year. You know, like 22s. A bitch to tie on to the leader."

"Pressure? What's that mean?"

"Pressure, means fishing pressure. Not too many people come down here to fish—at least not after opening day. Most fish upstream, closer to the dam. This is restricted fishing in here. See the sign over there? The white one on the tree? Fly Fishing Only. Catch and Release Only."

"Yeah. What does all that mean?"

"Means you can only fish with a fly rod, not a spinning rod, and you can only use artificial flies, no worms or bait, no spinner baits—metal spoons or metal spinners. And you put the fish back." O'Malley turned his head halfway around and tipped it up toward Vladimir. "You've never fished?"

"Never."

"Never in your whole life?"

"Never."

"Well, you should try it sometime." He turned his head away from Vladimir and leaned back toward the river. Both of them took a drag on their cigarettes. "See that. There was a rise out there." O'Malley pointed to a ring on the surface of the water. "Yup. A rise. That's for sure."

"A what?"

"Son, you got a lot to learn. It means when a fish, a trout, comes up to take a fly—to grab a fly to eat—that's when he makes that ring on the water. That's how you spot the fish, how you know where they are. How you know they're on the feed."

"Fly fishing. You have your own language. I'd need a dictionary to go fishing."

"Well, I never thought of it that way. Hey, Vlad—mind if I call you 'Vlad'?"

"No, not at all."

"Well, Vlad, let me ask you something. It's been a long time now, well, not that long, do you ever think about Constance Carmichael? Do you ever wonder what happened to her?"

"Well, not so much any more. Not really, I guess."

"But you knew her, didn't you?"

"Of course, I did. You know that."

O'Malley was now standing up looking at Vladimir. "She was one of your favorite little pals, wasn't she?"

"Yes. Of course, I knew her. But she wasn't exactly a 'friend.' I know all the girls in a casual way. I like all the girls at the school. That is sorta my job. Look, we've had this conversation before. Remember?"

"Sure, I remember. But, Constance, do you miss her?"

"Well, I suppose in a way I do. But there are always little girls at the school. They come and go. I like them all. They're all pretty much alike."

"I'm not believing that. Some of those little girls are, well, prettier than others. You couldn't help picking out favorites. That's a natural thing to do."

"You said that before. And, yes, I suppose I do have favorites. So what? But I am fond of them all. As I said before, and I suppose it sounds cruel, selfish, calloused, but somehow I really don't seem to miss Constance. I guess I know I suppose I should. Is that abnormal or something?"

"I don't know whether it's abnormal or not, maybe a bit strange being as you were, well, let's say close to her. I just thought you were more involved with her in particular."

Vladimir sat up straight. "'More involved with her?' What do you mean by that? That's not true. Why do you say it's 'strange' for me not to miss her"?

"Just because."

"So, P.J., do you think I'm strange?"

"Well, Vlad, I don't know. I don't really know you. Perhaps you're just being honest."

"Or what eccentric."

O'Malley dropped his cigarette to the ground and scrunched it with the toe of his wading boot. He turned toward Vladimir with a smile on his face.

"Well, Vlad, old lad, I don't know; I just don't know." Then with calculation, he said, "You seem like a pretty regular fellow to me. What makes you think you might deserve to be called eccentric?"

"It means that perhaps I am perceived to be a little odd. You know different from other people."

"Well, Vlad, we are all odd in some ways and all of us are different from other people. You and me, everybody, we're different individuals, and at the same time we're all alike."

Vladimir lay all the way back on the top of the car and cupped his hands behind his head; his legs were still hanging down through the sunroof. He was staring up at the canopy of limbs and leaves overhead.

"You know, P.J., I don't have a father. Did you know that? Oh, he's not dead or anything. It was a divorce. Maybe that's what makes me odd.

Maybe if I had a father I wouldn't be odd or different. More like everybody else. Maybe if I had a father he'd take me fishing. That would be more normal, a more normal thing. Wouldn't it?"

It was a warm day. O'Malley had unsnapped the suspenders on his chest waders and rolled the top of the waders down to his waist. At the question, with his body bent across the hood of the car, he scratched his chin.

"Let's look at this situation, lad. You got a father. We've all got fathers. Guess the trouble is, he just isn't here right now. But you had a father once, that's for sure. And, yes, it is normal for sons and fathers to go fishing together. Or to do other things together. I suppose that's true. But then, I never went fishing with my Pap."

"Never?"

"Never."

"Why was that?"

"We all worked too hard. Back in the Old Country, as they say, we had no time. Then we lived in New York, Manhattan, and there wasn't any place to go fishing. Anyway, again, not much time."

"But I don't really work at all. Never have. Is that odd, too?"

"No. Not odd, just lucky, I'd say. Why would you want to work if you didn't have to? If you had money, and you didn't need to make money. Hell, I don't think I'd have worked if I didn't have to. Hell, I don't work now. I'm retired. Basically, I got nothing to do all day, and, as I always say, it takes me all day to get it done."

"P.J., how many rods do you have?"

"O'Malley stood up and laughed. "Oh, I'd say too many. Way too many. Quite a collection. Maybe twelve."

"Twelve fishing rods?"

"Yep."

"Why so many? Do you have one or two favorites?"

"Well, you end up having so many because you're always *looking* for a favorite. Something better. Something bigger. Something smaller. You know, the right one, the perfect one. You kinda get tired of the same one; you want to try something different, something new. Besides they have all kinds of rods now. Keep changing and improving them. Used to be only bamboo, like this one here. Now they've got fiberglass, and lately, they've got, what's it called? Oh, graphite. But I prefer bamboo like this one. It's an Orvis bamboo. You see, Vlad, you need different lengths, too, and different weights. This one's a nine-footer for a 6 weight line. Got a little six-footer for small streams. Big rod, big fish, big water. Little rod, little fish, little water. Bet you're sorry you asked."

O'Malley reached for another cigarette. "Anglers are fickle guys when it comes to rods and fishing gear in general. That's the story, son. Yep, I got twelve fly rods. And like I just said, you need different rods, all shapes and sizes, same way you need different friends. Now, I'd guess a guy like you, a young man like you, you must have a lot of friends, a lot of different friends?"

"No. Matter of fact, I don't. Not really. I really don't have any friends. Well, I guess except the little girls at the school. And they're really not my friends. They are all pretty much alike, all pretty much the same."

"Well, that's OK I guess, if that's what you want."

"Yes, I suppose, but I'm beginning to think that it is not what I want. It's just the way it is."

"The way it is?"

"I don't know, P.J., never thought too much about it. Not until lately anyway. That's probably what makes me odd, playing around with little girls in a ballet school. My job, yeah. That's practically all I've ever known." Vladimir sat up. "You know what, P.J.? I'm beginning to wonder what a more, you know, a more 'normal' life would be like. You see, I don't think my life is normal. Vladimir lay back and looked up at the sky through the tree leaves. "P.J., Do you have children?"

"Yeah, a son and a daughter."

"I suppose they are grown up by now."

"Yes, all grown up now."

"Are you sad that they are all grown up? I mean I hate to see things grow up, don't you?"

"No, not sad. Proud."

"Did you take them fishing when they were children?"

"My daughter, she doesn't like it much. But Danny does. We go out West every summer. To Yellowstone. Fish the Big Horn in Montana, too."

O'Malley was amused. Here was this queer duck, ole Vladdy boy, interrogating *him* for Christ's sake. And he'd fallen into it. Vlad, it seemed, was calling the shots, and he was going along with it. Christ, was he getting soft? Had he lost his touch? "Oh, who the hell cared anyway?" he thought.

"What's Danny like? Your son."

"Oh, normal, I guess." They both laughed out loud. "Now you got me using that word."

"Hey, Vladdy," O'Malley straightened up, "oops, there I go again, that's a bad habit of mine, screwing around with people's names. Sorry, makes some people mad."

"I don't mind. Not at all."

"Well, let me ask *you* something for a change. It's about that watch of yours. Been admiring it. That's a Breitling, right? I see their ads in the *New York Times.* Seems they've always got one there. But I've never seen a real one up close. Seen Rolexes. Yeah. But never a Breitling. Could I take a closer look at it?"

"Sure." Vladimir sat up, extracted his legs from the sunroof and slid off the car. O'Malley noticed he had those buckled calfskin "kickers" on. They looked like he'd just polished them.

Now they were standing side-by-side, both with their bellies pressed against the front fender with their upper bodies bent over the hood propped up on their elbows. From that position, Vladimir took the watch off and handed it to O'Malley.

He turned it over, hefted it in the palm of his hand. "Whoa! it's even bigger and heavier than I thought. Jesus, Vlad, ole buddy, tell me about all this stuff, all these dials and gizmos. Do you know how to use them all?" He stood up and handed the watch back to Vladimir who stood up to receive it. Then they both leaned forward again on the hood of the car.

"Alright, P.J. It's not just *a* Breitling, it's a Breitling Montbrilliant Eclipse."

"Jesus, sounds like a French wine."

"It's an aviator's watch, a pilot's watch. The real thing. Used for navigation. See this." Vladimir put his long index finger on the outside bezel. "You can rotate this and it's a circular slide rule. You can use it to do multiplications and divisions. You can calculate distances, exchange rates, and stuff like that. For example—"

"Whoa! Hold it. You mean it's got a friggin' built-in slide rule?"

"Yes. Watch this. See that little red triangle? If I want to multiply 12 by, say, 2, or, let's make it harder, by 1,200, you turn this bezel like this. Now see that other red triangle? That's where the answer is. 144. Of course, you have to add the zeros. The answer is 14,400."

"Let me see that again." O'Malley held the watch in the palm of his hand as if it were the Hope diamond.

Vladimir looked over O'Malley's shoulder. "It has a chronograph module with a fifth of a second counter and a thirty-minute totalizer. Calculates the phases of the moon through its twenty-nine-and-a-half-day cycle and a—"

"Talk about needing a dictionary! That's enough. That's enough." O'Malley handed the watch back to Vladimir and held up the palms of his hands to the heavens. "Way outta my league, lad. You are way, way otta my league." They both laughed out loud.

When you have eliminated the impossible, what ever remains, however improbable, must be the truth.
— From *The Sign of Four* by Sir Arthur Conan Doyle

llen Sheffield, the tall, flirtatious ballet student, Vladimir's new favorite—she disappeared. It happened on a Thursday afternoon. Mrs. Sheffield had asked Ellen to walk home from the elementary school. When she realized that her daughter was a little late, that was, at first, no cause for alarm. Ellen had probably stopped off at the drugstore to hang out with friends. Besides Mrs. Sheffield was busy reviewing some new listings that she'd just picked up at the real estate office where she worked.

It was four o'clock before she looked up from her desk and realized that Ellen wasn't home. She went to the front door and looked down the street just as Elizabeth Carmichael had done on that cold dark day one year ago. And just as Elizabeth Carmichal had done, she called Grace at Carnaby's, thinking that Ellen might have stopped to chat with friends on the corner in front of the drugstore. By five o'clock she was seized by the same panic that had seized Elizabeth Carmichael. She called Corsetti. The pattern had begun to repeat itself in almost every detail.

This time Corsetti called O'Malley immediately.

"Patrick. It's happened again."

"What?"

"Ellen Sheffield, her mother, just called. Said she never came home from school."

"I'll come over."

Corsetti had an improvised ashtray on his desk by the time O'Malley got there.

"Make yourself at home Patrick because here we go again. Now, by God we have a pattern. Two girls nearly identical in age, well, I think Ellen is a bit younger. Same ballet school connection. Really weird, the same day, Thursday."

O'Malley picked up the pot from under the Krup coffeemaker and poured lukewarm coffee into a Styrofoam cup. He turned and looked over his shoulder toward Corsetti, "Is this the stuff with STP in it or that decaffeinated crap?"

"It's the real thing."

O'Malley sat down in the chair, placed the Styrofoam cup on Corsetti's desk, and lit a cigarette. "Yes, now we do have a pattern. But look, this disappearance, if that's what it is—after all it's only been several hours—bothers me. All along we've been assuming that some stranger came into town and kidnapped Constance. If we do have another disappearance here, I don't think it's very likely that a stranger would come to *this* town again. He'd go to another town. Maybe one of the other towns, up river or down river. Unless, of course, the kidnapper lives right here. At first, with Constance, I thought we had a random abduction. Now I'm not so sure. Now the pattern looks like this person might live right here in the village."

"Look, Patrick, either it is someone who lives in town or our mysterious stranger decided that Croton made easy pickings and he returned."

"That's possible. But I'm not so sure he'd do that. I think he'd be long gone. He wouldn't hang around. Now I'm thinking we have some bad egg right here in the village. Close people—neighbors, husbands, uncles, in general, they commit most crimes, people like that who live with or near the victim. People who know the victim."

"But we've been thinking it was a stranger, a random thing. If it is the same person …" Corsetti said. "Look, after Constance disappeared, we went through this village with a fine-tooth comb. We looked everywhere for clues, talked with everyone, and found nothing, absolutely nothing and no credible suspects—we didn't narrow it down to a single prime suspect. It's all the same again. There's still no suspect, no apparent motive other than what we talked about the last time, 'pedophilia?'"

"You're learning but you're jumping to conclusions again. Besides this one is only four hours old. Let's hope it's not the same thing. Let's hope she stopped off at a friend's."

"There's been no phone call. So what else could it be?" said Corsetti. "Can't be, as you've said a classic motive. Who would have anything against a schoolgirl? Who could get that mad at a schoolgirl? No, Patrick, it's—I know it in my bones—it's another abduction. Who else but a child molester would make a child disappear?"

"Whoa." O'Malley walked up to Corsetti and clamped his hands on the man's shoulders. "Calm down, pal. We don't even know if Constance was murdered. Let alone what happened to this girl who's been missing for only about four hours? You know damn well she could have stopped off at a friend's house. Let's not go through this whole thing again."

"Patrick, I am not going to crap around with this one. No more seminars, no waiting. We're getting out in the street right away."

"Fine. I agree with you. But the last thing we want to do is jump to conclusions. Panic. Besides—classic motives are out—Jesus, now you've got me jumping to conclusions. What th' hell's the matter with me? Talking about murder four hours after a little girl fails to come home from school. So, here we go again, and all we can do is investigate, wait, and speculate."

Days passed, then weeks and Ellen was still gone. The investigation began as it had in the case of Constance's disappearance. All the same bases were touched, all the same places searched, all the same people questioned. There was a pattern but there was no pattern.

The pressure on Corsetti and his friend O'Malley became intense. As before, the state police and the F.B.I were involved. But all the panic, anger, and impatience in the village focused on Corsetti and O'Malley. In the village, there was practically no other topic of conversation. Where there had been just ordinary news coverage of Constance's disappearance, the story of Ellen's disappearance was everywhere. It went out on the AP wire. All the newspapers and the TV networks picked it up. Reporters and cameramen swarmed into the village. The fact that this had happened twice in the sleepy little village of Croton-on-Hudson was news, big news. Just the kind of news people love because it shatters the complacency of the comfortable, law-abiding suburban middle class.

"For Christ's sake," O'Malley thought, "I'm retired. I don't need this. Not again." Corsetti himself was now only a few years away from retirement. He didn't need this either. Not again.

The last time the two men had covered—at least they thought they had—every possible angle. This time was no different. They investigated every possibility. They looked everywhere, sought help and advice from everyone in the law enforcement community. Done everything. The ballet school connection seemed to loom larger now, but actually there was no more reason to suspect a real connection to the ballet school than there was to suspect a real connection to the elementary school. That was probably a coincidence. But that's what patterns are all about. Besides, both those angles had been, then and now, thoroughly investigated. Each and every other "angle"—close friends, family—had been put under the microscope. Even more so now.

There was no apparent dysfunction of any kind in either the Carmichael or the Sheffield families. They were typical in every detail of the well-educated, white-collar Crotonites, executive and professionals yo-yoing down to New York and back to Croton everyday. Neither the Carmichaels nor the Sheffields were large extended families. No relatives lived with them nor did they have any relatives living in town or nearby. Therefore, neither family had a cluster of possible child molesters—uncles, grandfathers—interacting with them. Besides, as O'Malley had observed, relatives may molest children in the family, but they don't abduct and kill them. They don't have to.

Even though they ruled out family members, they still thought the kidnapper probably was someone living in the village. Someone the children knew. And trusted. It is hard to imagine that either Constance or Ellen would get into a car with a stranger. Although very young, they were nonetheless sophisticated children. Not naïve hicks. Both were their parents' only child. Spoiled and pampered, they lived in an adult world. They were treated like adults. It is very unlikely that a psychopathic stranger, no matter how persuasive and charming, could have conned them. They were too smart for that. Too smart to fall for the "help me find my dog" trick.

Yet, clearly, that is precisely what happened. They were somehow persuaded to get into a car. Both were out walking. One was walking home from school, the other walking down to the drugstore. Something kids do all the time in this town. Someone had to persuade them to get into a car. Accept a lift. But all the distances were so short, unless the children knew and trusted the *someone* in the car, they would have little motivation to accept a ride.

Teachers, priests, coaches, close family friends, even a member of the immediate family, or the mother or father of a friend are all possible suspects, if one is talking about child molestation. But again O'Malley and Corsetti and the other investigators that considered the circumstances of the girls' disappearances felt that those kinds of people are also unlikely to kidnap their victims or murder them. Yes, some uncle becomes enamored with his niece and he may persuade her to accompany him on a cross-country journey … like the situation in Nabokov's *Lolita*.

The parish board, the lay leaders at the Holy Name of Mary Church, where both girls attended, had, on their own initiative, reviewed the background of their pastors to assure themselves that the priests' records were clean. And they were. Completely. They had even hired a counselor for the Carmichaels, and he had helped other parishioners warn their children about the signs of child abuse. Warned the children about the dangers of accepting rides from strangers. Other counselors had been hired to talk to the children at Carrie E. Thompson Elementary School. The community had taken all the steps it could think of to guard against a recurrence.

In the case of Ellen's disappearance, the village was faced, for all practical purposes, with a perfect parallel. Repeat: a *perfect parallel*. This was good in the sense that the investigators now had their long–sought-for pattern; bad in the sense that unless there were clues this time, the investigation would be going over plowed ground. A complete Constance redux. They were right back where they started.

This time, however, O'Malley thought more deeply about the possible dance-school connection. What could the dance school possibly have to do with it? What could the regal and aloof Mrs. Petrovsky and her son Vladimir possibly have to do with any of this. Was it a coincidence that the two girls just happened to be enrolled at that school? Now as before he could not think about the dance school without thinking about that "queer duck," Vladimir.

Ever since Constance disappeared, O'Malley had started reading about ballet in the dance section of the Sunday *Times'* entertainment section, which was the largest, most colorful section of the gigantic Sunday edition. It always covered "Dance" and under "Dance," "Ballet." What he discovered was an exotic world filled with fairies, butterflies, swans, and beautiful, really beautiful young women.

He learned to admire the athleticism and discipline that dance, especially ballet, required, and in his reading he learned that the world of dance at the professional level was perhaps no more strange or libertine than other areas of the arts. His reading introduced him to the *faux-naif* sexuality that seems to pervade ballet. "It is," he thought, "very often high-class burlesque—a grand and elaborate titillation and tease."

Now, after the disappearance of Ellen, having filled his head with this superficial knowledge of, if not appreciation for, ballet, he felt that he had an advantage; he had an edge as far as the dance school was concerned. What's more, he had made a connection with Vladimir that would make it easier this time. So he called Vladimir and played the friendship card.

"Hello, Vlad. O'Malley here. I was wondering, could I come over and talk to you?"

"Of course. Yes, when? Do I need to know what you want to talk about or should I guess. My God. How can this have happened again?"

"You guessed it. Let's put our heads together. Like Constance, you knew Ellen. You may know something you don't know you know. Anyway, I'm on my way over. I really need your help."

"I cannot imagine how I could help you."

"I said I'm on my way and when I get there, I'll tell you."

"O'Malley, look, please, this is just like the last time when we talked about Constance. I don't know any more now than I knew then. Again, I don't know *anything*."

"Look, Vladimir, just talking to you, kicking around ideas, picking your brains, that could help. You knew both these girls and you might know something you don't realize you know. C'mon, do me a favor."

"Alright. Come on over. It's Thursday. The school's closed any way. Mrs. Petrovsky is not here. She's out. At the Fletcher's. This would be a good time."

"I'll be right over. Put the coffee pot on."

O'Malley arrived twenty minutes later and Vladimir answered the door. In spite of the circumstances, he had a smile on his face as if he were genuinely glad to see the old detective. This time there was a more accepting and casual atmosphere between the two men. This time Vladimir appeared to be more interested, ready to be more analytical, more helpful.

This time, like chums, they sat down and lit up cigarettes in the parlor of the Funderburk mansion. O'Malley told Vladimir right off that he didn't want to sit in that damn horse-collar chair so Vladimir brought out a straight-backed chair from the other room. Vladimir sat on the desk chair as before.

O'Malley began by asking all the routine questions: any strangers, any cars parked along the street, anything strange about Ellen's behavior prior to that Thursday when she disappeared? Is there any significance to Thursday or is that a coincidence, too? Is the ballet school always closed on Thursdays?

"Can you think of anything, Vladdy, anything that might help us?"

Vladimir could think of nothing. Even his flirtations with Ellen, which he would never reveal to O'Malley, or anyone else for that matter, appeared in his mind to be completely unremarkable and irrelevant. He had only lately begun to feel some faint intimations of guilt about the games he had played with those two girls. But he could not imagine that that had anything whatsoever to do with their disappearance. They were just games, mere amusements. They caused no harm.

"No," said Vladimir. "I can still think of nothing unusual. Are there still no clues?"

"To tell you the truth, absolutely nothing. Ellen, like Constance, has disappeared into thin air. Without a trace."

"Do you think they were both murdered?"

"Vladimir, we don't even know that. We never give up hope until we find a body; until then they are missing persons. Period."

The conversation wound its way through thoughts and conjectures. Another small seminar as Corsetti would impatiently say. O'Malley made the appearance of taking Vladimir into his confidence. He was making him a partner in the investigation, complimenting him on his few conjectures, and hypotheticals. Then he brought up the real purpose of his visit.

"Hey, Vlad, I was in here once when the Funderburks owned it. Just once. Can't remember why. Looks like you've done some extensive remodeling, changed things around a great deal. Why don't you give me a tour?"

"A tour?"

"Yeah, show me around the place. Show me what you've done to it."

"Well, Mrs. Petrovsky, she supervised everything. Drove the workers crazy. The architect—Tate, the guy in town," he laughed, "she drove him and the contractors absolutely crazy, too. But I'm not sure you're really interested in the decorations and renovations. I think you want to take a look around as part of the investigation, right?"

"It wouldn't take a genius to figure that out," O'Malley answered.

"Look, O'Malley, old pal, as you'd say, you've asked all the classic questions, haven't you? And I suppose I should give you the classic answer, which is 'We have nothing to hide.' If Mrs. Petrovsky or I had anything to hide, then I'd say, 'better get a search warrant.'"

O'Malley knew he did not have sufficient grounds for a search warrant. Usually that takes some piece of concrete evidence plus probable cause. There was no evidence, not one shred of evidence to implicate either Vladimir, or, for God's sake, Mrs. Petrovsky. But if there were evidence, it would not take an NYPD detective to surmise that it might be found here.

This is the one thing, damn it, that he had not done before. And that was a mistake. Now all he could do was hope Vladimir would let him just walk through the house. Without a warrant. He was suspicious as hell. Vladimir was the kind of strange, eccentric type who could, indeed, be a monster in disguise. He had that superficial charm that all con men and serial killers seem to have. He could, by God, be the one. If only O'Malley could find some bit of evidence, even some faint circumstantial evidence, anything to hang his hat on.

"OK, buddy," said O'Malley, "be a hard ass if you want to. But, get this straight. Everything I do is part of the investigation. You know that. What I'm looking for is to learn something more about the girls' routine, something that might give me some common link between the disappearance of Constance and the disappearance of Ellen. Look, it's entirely up to you. But I know you want to help. Isn't that true?"

"Yes, of course, I want to help, but I don't see how traipsing through our home, invading our privacy, could possibly help. The girls only come here for dance lessons, downstairs over there. The dance floor, the barre. There's no routine except that. They come in with their dance bags, go to the changing room, change into leotards or tights, come out, dance, and go home."

"Don't they ever go upstairs?" O'Malley turned and looked toward the stairs.

"Oh, God," thought Vladimir, "wait till he sees all that crap in my room."

But that was the way it was, so he said, "Yes, of course, on occasion they do. Sometimes, when Mrs. Petrovsky wants to concentrate on several select girls, you know teach them a certain part, and the others have nothing to do for a while, they go upstairs. That happens. But they don't have free-run of the house. I always go with them. I supervise them. I entertain them. That's my job. I have toys and games for them, yes, upstairs, or I take them out into the garden to look at the flowers."

"Come on, Vladimir. You know this kind of thing is routine."

"Routine? What kind of thing?"

"Asking to take a look around. Let's do it this way, the informal way. It will make it easier on both of us."

"Routine, yes, P.J., old pal, when a detective suspects someone. Then it's routine. May I ask, even though I know the answer, do you suspect me?"

"Yes, I do, of course, I do. You are obviously a 'person of interest' just as you were last time. Yes, I suspect anyone and everyone, everyone who has ever been here. Anyone who's repaired a faucet or fixed a light. I suspect everyone, God damn it. Everyone in town. Even the girls' parents. Their fathers. Their neighbors. Everyone. That can't surprise you and obviously doesn't. Look, pal, outside of family and friends, you probably had the closest connection with these two girls." O'Malley felt his cheeks flush.

"No, it does not surprise me. That's true. But I am no fool. Perhaps, it's time for the Petrovskys to get themselves a lawyer."

"I can get this out of the way right now, Vladdy. Do you want me to do that? Want me to stop pussyfooting around with you? Want me to ask you the question? Is that what you want? Let's stop being cute with each other."

"Go ahead. Ask the question."

"OK. Did you have anything whatsoever to do with the disappearance of Constance Carmichael or Ellen Sheffield?

"No. Absolutely not."

"Do you know anyone who might have a motive for abducting them or doing them harm?

"No. Absolutely not."

"OK, now that's out of the way. Look, Vladimir, I am not *searching* for anything in particular. I don't know what I'm looking for. Am I looking for clues? Of course, I am. I am always looking for clues. And remember this, Vlad, this isn't just a home; it is a school. Why should you be exempt? Corsetti and I searched the Carmichael's home and the Sheffield's home. *Searched* their homes. Not so much because we suspected them but to look for any possible clue that would shed light on the girls' disappearance.

Diaries, notes, whatever. Anything that might sharpen our intuitions. But, right, I don't have a search warrant. "

Vladimir knew that to deny O'Malley's request, even to go though the song and dance he had just gone through, would only increase O'Malley's suspicions. What was his real concern anyway?

Vladimir felt that he had built some sort of simpatico relationship with O'Malley, some faint man-to-man camaraderie. So his real concern was the condition of his upstairs living room. All those toys, dolls, games, and children's books. This might be hard to explain if not embarrassing. He really did not want O'Malley to think of him as some kind of freak. Some kind of sissy. He knew O'Malley already thought he was odd, and he didn't want to reinforce that perception. Besides O'Malley had said that we are all different if not odd in some way. So to hell with it. He could not change O'Malley's view of him. What the hell, he *was* odd. Genuinely odd. He knew that. Besides that, he had already told O'Malley that he would, as part of his "job," entertain the girls upstairs or out in the garden. So what's the harm? This is a fucking school for children. And children play with toys.

"Yes, Mr. O'Malley, I understand. I understand perfectly well. I know exactly what you are doing, what you have to do. It is your job. I do know that Mrs. Petrovsky would not approve. She would certainly call our lawyer. But that's another thing. That's my problem. Come on, detective, I'll give you a Cook's tour of the Petrovsky School of Classical Ballet, upstairs and downstairs."

O'Malley had not realized just how big this house was, how full of nooks and crannies. Even if he had a search warrant, it would be a big job to go through it. And, speaking of intuition, he did know how Vladimir must feel about having somebody tromping through his private world. No, it wasn't sympathy that O'Malley felt. He just knew how he'd feel in Vladimir's place. But either out of true respect for Vladimir's sensibilities or out of a wish to protect the rapport he had so carefully built with him; he would try to make the walk-through as casual and non-threatening as possible. Although it would be a task particularly difficult for O'Malley, he would also try to keep his fuckin' mouth shut. That, for O'Malley would take a supreme act of will power. "Well, here we go," he thought. "Another chance for me to see how the other half lives."

"This way, inspector," said Vladimir with a theatrical bow and a swish of his hand.

Vladimir led him directly upstairs to his suite. Why not? What the hell?

O'Malley was amazed, if not slightly amused, by the twin suites. As for the clutter of toys, he had seen far weirder things rummaging through apartments on the Upper East Side. So Vladimir's array of children's books and toys, even the dolls, didn't really surprise him. Given the nature of the school, the toys up there were not that inappropriate. It was, after all, a little girl's school and this room was equipped like a waiting room at let's say an upscale pediatrician's office. You cater to your clients. It was a place where Vladimir entertained his mother's clients, and they were child ballerinas, so no big deal.

O'Malley was, however, absolutely astonished at the size and lavishness of the combined bathrooms. He had never seen anything like it. Not even on Park Avenue. He recognized the little inset Sub-Zero refrigerators. "Didn't know they made them that small. Jesus," he thought, "sippin' an ice-cold brewskie while you're soaking in the tub! This has to be the height of luxury." But he said nothing out loud.

Vladimir walked across the tile floor and opened the door to Mrs. Petrovsky's bedroom. O'Malley peered in. Sensing that Vladimir was not inviting him to enter, he hesitated. But then he went in anyway. The curtains were open and O'Malley was struck by the brightness of the room in contrast to Vladimir's curtained play parlor.

O'Malley saw nothing to arouse his suspicions. It was all in keeping with the décor throughout the house. When he finished his walkabout, Vladimir closed the door to Mrs. Petrovsky's rooms, and he and O'Malley retraced their steps through the bathroom, walked across the play parlor, and opened the door to his bedroom. He stood aside so that O'Malley could enter.

The bed was made and multicolored pillows were stacked against the headboard. Everything else was tucked in and tidy. There were no dolls or Teddy bears on the bed. Or anywhere in the room. In fact, the room looked masculine—maroons and browns—in rather sharp contrast to the other rooms and in spite of its general décor. O'Malley did notice the vase of flowers on the bedside table. "Nice touch," he thought. Although it was now mid-afternoon, the flowers were still there. Mrs. Spertano just couldn't bring herself to throw them away, at least not first thing in the morning. They were too fresh to be thrown away. So in spite of Mrs. Petrovsky's specific instructions, she left them there. "If she wants to throw away perfectly good flowers," thought Mrs. Spertano, "then let her do it herself." An act of civil disobedience done in the name of beauty.

O'Malley had asked no questions as they passed from room to room. Vladimir made no comments. O'Malley took no notes, at least not with pad and pencil. He saw nothing to arouse his suspicions. In fact, Vladimir's off-hand manner and casualness decreased his suspicions. He appeared very calm. He had been honest about how Mrs. Petrovsky would view this intrusion … and the price he himself might pay for it. Another act of civil disobedience, this one probably in the name of, well, simpatico.

"Where does that go," said O'Malley, finally breaking his vow of silence, pointing to the attic door.

"The attic," Vladimir answered. "Want to go up?"

"What's up there?"

"Do you know, P.J., I've only been up there once. We don't store anything up there. Mrs. Petrovsky had so many closets and such large ones built in downstairs and in the suites, we just don't need the storage space. All that's up there—all I remember—are mostly some old trunks."

"OK, let's have a look. Do you mind?" O'Malley asked.

"No. Not in the least," Vladimir reached for the doorknob and pulled the door open. "Go on up. See for yourself, Sherlock." O'Malley stepped around Vladimir and walked up the steps.

"Hey, where's the light switch? Is it down there?"

"No, it's up there. Should be a cord hanging down right there where you're standing."

As his eyes got used to the dark, he looked up over his head. Then felt around. "Got it."

He smelled mothballs as he looked around the room. All he saw were trunks, old-fashioned ones. And, in the back, in the yellow light from the single bulb, he could see two wicker clothes hampers and beside them two large, tall, upright trunks—portmanteaus.

"You're right. Nothing much but some old trunks." He pulled the cord and shuffled back down the steps in the dark.

Before he left, Vladimir took him into the basement. Like the attic it was untouched by the renovations. Unlike the attic it was empty except for a laundry hamper, washer, dryer, and utility sink. Nothing was stored there.

At the front door, O'Malley said, "Thanks. I appreciate it."

"My pleasure, Mr. Sherlock," replied Vladimir smiling.

O'Malley stepped out onto the porch, paused, and turned around. "Now tell me, Vladimir, where did you hide the bodies?"

Vladimir smiled broadly and said, "Why under my bed."

O'Malley laughed.

I need love more than ever now. . . I need your love,
I need love more than hope or money, wisdom or a
drink. . . .

— From *This Is My Beloved* by Walter Benton

On the Thursday afternoon of O'Malley's house tour—Mrs. Petrovsky's day off—she came home later than usual. Too late to see O'Malley leaving the mansion. She was not very pleased when Vladimir told her about his visitor. Especially not pleased with the revelation that Vladimir had allowed the detective, "that lout," to wander around her home. "Good, God, did you take him into my bedroom; show him my bathroom? Did he have a search warrant? I think *not*. What w*ere* you thinking? It's bad enough to have him asking us questions."

Having a stranger, particularly that odious Irishman, view all of her precious things, invade her private, personal world, was an uncomfortable thought for Mrs. Petrovsky. She told Vladimir just that in no uncertain terms. Letting O'Malley, that slob of all people, violate her privacy, my God, in doing that he had done "an irresponsible, and very stupid thing. If he suspects us of anything, then let him go and get a search warrant."

She sulked around the house for hours. Then locked herself in her upstairs parlor. Refused to eat supper. Before she went to bed, rather before she went to sleep, Vladimir spoke to her through her bedroom door. He said that he was sorry, really very, very sorry. Of course, he didn't mean it. And he smiled.

29

Do you want music without ears, scents without a nose, sights without eyes, a bed without love?
— From *By Grand Central Station I Sat Down and Wept*
by Elizabeth Smart

Several days after O'Malley's visit, Vladimir, readying himself for bed, entered the play parlor from his bedroom and walked over to the little refrigerator. He opened the door and took out a bottle of Perrier spring water. While drinking the water, he noticed that the door to the attic was ajar. His fault, he thought. Probably left it that way after O'Malley was up there.

"Now that's a perfect invitation for the girls to sneak up there when I'm not looking," he thought. Not that he thought any one of them had the spunk to go up there without his permission. Little boys, maybe, but not little girls. He decided to look around anyway. Yes, if the girls had gotten up there, he'd better have a look around. He walked over to the door, grabbed the doorknob, and pulled it open all the way.

He climbed the stairs and felt around in the dark for the light cord. When he found it and pulled it, he realized that to reach the cord you would have to be taller than a little ballerina, even taller than Ellen. He hadn't noticed that before because it was O'Malley who had gone up the steps and pulled the cord.

It was a typical attic—dust and cobwebs. Although he said he had, he had never really been up there. Dust made him wheeze and sneeze. He knew about the trunks only because Mrs. Petrovsky had once remarked that she'd seen them and wished that Funderburks had cleaned out the attic and taken those trunks and old clothes with them.

He could see the trunks well enough in the light of that single bare bulb. They were old and outdated, antiques. No one used trunks like that anymore. No wonder they left them. He fought back the urge to sneeze.

He noticed the two portmanteaus standing side-by-side against the back wall. "What monstrosities they are!" he thought. He wondered if they had any clothes in them. If they did that would explain the odor of mothballs.

He walked over to them, bent over, and tried the latch on one of them. Locked. The other. Locked also. He realized that he was now standing directly over Mrs. Petrovsky's suite, right over her bedroom. She was downstairs in the kitchen when he last saw her, but she would be coming upstairs any minute. She would be angry if she thought for a minute that he had been careless enough to let the girls come up here.

"What the hell," he thought, "they couldn't get hurt up here anyway... well, unless a trunk fell over on one of them."

When he came down and closed the door, he noticed that there was no keyhole beneath the doorknob. If there had been, he'd have gotten a skeleton key and locked the door. Instead, he closed it, tugged on the knob and turned it several times to make sure the latch was engaged.

He went into his side of the bathroom, stripped, turned on the shower, and scrubbed the dust and smell of mothballs off his skin.

In bed that night, he began to focus, perhaps for the first time, in a critical way on his life with Mrs. Petrovsky. It was comfortable. It truly was. Absolutely. He didn't have to think about much of anything. As O'Malley said, he was lucky not to have to really go to work. He just had to live. Play with pretty little girls and flowers. Sleep and eat. That's about all.

But he wondered what a different kind of life would be like, a more, let's say, normal kind of life; a life with his father, for example. What would that be like? Perhaps, he didn't like this life as much as he once thought he did. He'd done things in this life—things he was ashamed of, things that he would not have done in a different kind of life. Under different circumstances.

What would it be like? Life with his father? His father would work somewhere on weekdays, but on weekends perhaps they'd go over to the clay courts behind the high school for a game of tennis. Or maybe they'd go fishing. He wondered if he'd like that, if he'd like fishing. He thought he would. Fly fishing especially. Of course, it would be fly-fishing. His father, both he and his father, they would have Orvis rods, bamboo, like O'Malley's, not a dozen but several, and Hardy reels to go with them. Or maybe they'd go sailing on the Hudson. Of course, they'd have their own sailboat. Yes, probably a sailboat, not a motor boat. Well, maybe it would be a motorboat, a grand and gleaming vintage Chris-Craft. That would be nice. With the finest mahogany decks, varnished teak trim, polished brass, and chrome fittings and a windshield. In a boat like that they could take a trip together, a day trip up the Hudson River, go all the way to West Point. It would be a warm but breezy day in early June. They'd bring their lunch in that wicker picnic hamper of his or tie up at the Stone Mountain marina and have lunch at the Stone Mountain Tavern.

He'd never been there. But he knew about it. He'd been to the park once but had never been inside the tavern. That's what they'd do. They'd have drinks. His father would order a Beefeater Martini with a twist. He'd have a beer, a Heineken or Bass Ale, and they'd have BLT sandwiches. Or maybe a big bacon cheeseburger with lettuce, sliced tomato, and mayonnaise oozing out the sides. Mrs. Petrovsky thought them gross. But my father and I would eat a big BLT or burger and blot our lips with paper napkins and smile and talk about the wonderful day we were having.

Then, he thought, "hey, I know what I should do? I should ask P. J. O'Malley to take me fishing. Fly-fishing on the Croton River. You know, just to get a taste of it."

He fell asleep. Smiling.

No man chooses evil not because it is evil; he only mistakes it for happiness, the good he seeks.
— From *A Vindication of the Rights of Men* by Mary Wollstonecraft Godwin

Vladimir pulled his Jaguar up in front of 62 Morningside Drive at precisely 10:32:15 a.m., according to his Breitling. O'Malley was sitting on the side porch in his bathrobe and black leather grandfather slippers reading the *New York Times* and drinking a mug of coffee.

O'Malley saw the car pull up out of the corner of his eye and remained seated.

Vladimir swung his legs out of the car, closed the door with a loud thunk, and walked up the flagstone walk, dodging along the way an open can of dried up paint, a rake, and a shovel.

O'Malley scrunched the paper down like an accordion into his lap. "Well, who's this? Why it's Vladimir, Vladimir Petrovsky. The very same. What a pleasant surprise. What are you up to, lad?"

Vladimir stopped with one foot poised on the first porch step. "Thought you might have an extra cup of coffee?"

O'Malley put the paper down on the little wicker table beside his chair, picked up his mug, and said, "Well, by God, I do. A whole pot at that. Pull up a chair. I'll go in and get you a mug of hot coffee. Cream, sugar, or both?"

"None of the above."

O'Malley picked up his mug, kicked the screen door open with his foot, and went into the kitchen. He came back with two mugs filled to the brim with coffee. He handed one to Vladimir and sat back in his chair. "Well, what's up?"

"Nothing. Just bored, I guess."

"Well, if you're bored, you've come to the right place, welcome to Boredom Manor. I'm bored, too. So now what do we do?" O'Malley picked up the pack of Camels on the table, pulled one out, and lit it with a match. "Smoke? Oh, I remember, you smoke those fancy Tareytons."

Vladimir slapped his shirt pocket. It was empty. "No, I mean, yes. Forgot mine. I'll try one of yours."

"Mind you, there's no filter. Are you up for that?"

"Yeah, I know. That's OK"

"Here then have a Camel. That's what real men smoke." O'Malley handed him the pack then leaned back stretched his legs out and spread them. He was wearing blue-striped pajamas under his bathrobe. "OK," he said, locking his fingers and cupping his hands behind his head, "pick a topic of conversation. Guest's choice. There's nothing I can't talk about ... intelligently. My knowledge of everything is a mile wide and an inch deep."

Vladimir patted his trouser pocket. He forgot his Ronson, too. He picked up O'Malley's pack of matches, lit the Camel, and said, "How about life?"

"Whoa. Life? Now that's a pretty broad topic. You've got to narrow it down."

"OK, let's see." Vladimir leaned back in the chair, spread his legs out, and took a drag off his cigarette. "Your life. What it's like to be a big city detective?"

"Ah, Vlad, excellent choice. I love to talk, and my favorite subject is myself. But I'm retired now. So, now, being a big city detective is like this," he gestured across the porch with his hand. "It's like this … getting up late, sitting around in my bathrobe, reading books, reading the papers, getting the junk mail out of the box, leaving my stuff all over the lawn. Oh, and calling the kids. Listening to the river crawl by. *Listen.* You can hear it now. That's about it. You see, Vladdy, I really do have nothing to do."

"Neither do I. Guess that makes me 'retired.' You could say I was *born* retired. Lately that's all I've ever done it seems: Nothing."

"That's a lucky way to be born, pal."

"I think I'm getting tired of it." Vladimir took a sip of coffee.

"Then go out and get yourself a job. Take a trip. Go back to school. You're right, you can't just sit around doing nothing all the time unless you're old like me. You're too young for that."

"But that's what *you* do."

"Didn't you hear the words 'old like me?' You see, Vladdy, I got a whole life *behind* me, lots of memories, good ones and bad. Besides, read my lips, I'm *old* now, tired, haven't got the energy I once had. So for an old geezer like me it's OK to sit around and think and read, fetch the mail and go fishing. Get to my age and you'll feel the same way. First, you go get a life; then you go live it, live it fast or live it slow, and when you can't climb the stairs any more, you sit down and relax. Can't really do one without the other. Can't retire from retirement. Ah, retirement, well, it's something you earn, usually. Like when you've run the races, and they put you out to pasture. Yeah, I earned it. Now I'm out to pasture."

"Me, I'm not good at remembering. Haven't really got that much to remember."

"That's 'cause you're young. You've got the school. You've got a job there. Helping Mrs. Petrovsky. Doesn't that keep you busy?"

"No, not really. I'm just sort of hanging around."

"Vlad, it's my turn, now, my turn to pick a topic. Let's talk about those girls again."

"Not again. Please. Not again. Is that all you ever think about? Come on. Let it go. You're retired. Why do you care anyway? What's that got to do with you and your life in retirement? Besides, P.J., *which* girls? You'll have to narrow it down."

"Smart ass. Takin' a page outta of my book, are you? OK, that's fair. Constance and Ellen. Your old friends. The girls who fucked up my retirement. You're right, that's all I ever think about. How about you? Don't you ever think about them?"

"No. Not any more. Not really."

"Don't you care? For Christ's sake, you knew them, played with them!"

"Please, O'Malley. Let's drop it. We've had this conversation before. I thought you could, you said, you said you could talk about everything and anything but this is all you want to talk about. Just because I don't think about it doesn't mean I don't care. I do care. But I try *not* to think about it. I've practiced forgetting things all my life. You should try that. What is it with you anyway?"

"Yeah, you're right. I supposed I do think about it way too much. It's a bitch. One big bitch. But, God dammit, that's what a detective does. I can't just turn it off. Yeah, I never stop wondering where they are, what happened to them."

"This is what you do? Even in retirement? Is that all you do, ask questions and look for bodies?"

"What?" O'Malley drew his legs in and turned. "Why do you say that? Why do you say, 'Look for bodies?'"

"Because that's true. Because they're dead. You know that. You know that's what everybody thinks … even if they don't say so. Everybody thinks those girls are dead. Now all you have to do is find the bodies."

"That's not true. Ask Elizabeth Carmichael. She'll tell you that she knows her daughter will come home some day. If it were my daughter, that's the way I'd feel. But, yes, you're right, detectives do look for bodies … all the while, in cases like this, praying that they never find them. Praying that things like this will never happen."

"Then is this a perfect crime? Two perfect crimes." Vladimir said.

O'Malley looked supremely sad, "I like to believe that there is no such thing. But to tell the truth, there are. Especially when it comes to missing children. Many of these cases are never solved. *Never.* We don't like to publicize that, but it's true. Oh, sometimes, lots of times, even after a couple of years, bodies are found and the criminal is caught. Sometimes it might take ten years or more. These cases are never closed."

"So murderers get away with murder?"

"That's the story kid. Shit happens."

"They were just little girls, " said Vladimir."

"Just little girls? How can you say that? Look, pal, I have a daughter. I can imagine how the mothers and fathers feel. Makes it worse that they were children. A damn shame. And it's a damn shame whether they were little girls, big boys, old men, or bow-legged women; remember in God's world, everybody counts."

Was Vladimir playing a game of cat and mouse with him? Why the hell had he come over there in the first place? O'Malley wondered. Vladimir was assuming they were murdered, did that mean he knew something? Oh, of course not. Everyone else thought the same thing. But how could you not think that he might be playing a game that's often played between perpetrators and detectives. That's not unusual in cases like this. But Vladimir seemed so genuinely forthright, even naive about this whole thing. He really wasn't thinking about the girls disappearance all that much, not because he was callous but because he was, well, self-centered. He was focusing on other things. Like his own life. He was just a laconic, confused kid who'd been born with a silver spoon in his mouth and now didn't care about much of anything. Except maybe changing his own life.

"You're the one who asked me how I think about this, how a detective thinks about things like this. Are you really interested?"

"No, not really," said Vladimir.

"Then why'd you ask?"

"Because I'm bored."

"That's flattering. I thought you wanted to know all about my life as a big city detective. Know what, I'm bored with the whole thing, too." O'Malley slapped his palms down on his thighs. "Time to change the subject."

"May I have another cigarette?" Vladimir got up and stretched. Arching his back he leaned his backside on the porch railing.

"Sure, grab one. What? You want me to deliver it? Tell me, Vladdy, why always the white shirt and black pants. Maybe you should become a priest. You got the clothes for it."

"Fewer decisions in the morning. And, you, what about you, why the pajamas? Is that why they call you 'P.J.' Because you go around ..."

"Very funny, father Petrovsky. My answer's the same as yours—fewer decisions. Just roll out and put my feet on the floor."

"Go ahead. Talk about the girls if you want to," said Vladimir.

"But you said you're not interested."

"And I'm not. But *you* are."

"Yeah. But I'm weary of the topic. Wish I didn't care anymore. Try not to. Besides there isn't really much to talk about. No evidence. No witnesses. No leads. No bodies. No motive."

"Motive?"

"Yeah, the big *why*? Why did someone want this to happen? Who made it happen? Some fucking pervert, some pedophile that comes into town and steals two little girls. Christ, I'm sick to death of talking about it. Sick of the whole damn thing."

"Pedophile?"

"Don't you know that word? People who have an abnormal attraction to children. A *sexual* attraction."

"You mean that's what happened here? This was a sexual ... But why kill?"

"Where have you been, kid? To the cover up their crime. No body, no crime. He doesn't want to get caught. He knows what he's done is evil. In other types of crimes, the killing itself is the goal. It's done to remove some obstacle to the killer's happiness. It's done impulsively in passion, in a rage. It's a response to, well, rejection. A wife asks for a divorce. Husband goes berserk and kills his wife, all the kids, and himself. Guys like that don't hide bodies.

"I've spent twenty years crawling through this muck. Now I can't crawl out of it. That's right, kid. I've become a broken record ... saying the same thing over and over again, singing the same song." O'Malley ground out his Camel in the ashtray.

"Why do these things happen?" asked Vladimir.

"They happen because people go around wanting someone else to do something that *they want them to do*. When that doesn't happen, they get pissed. Give me my money back, you S.O.B. or I'm gonna mess you up. Give me my job back or else. Do what I want you to do or pay the consequences. Half the angst in the world is caused by this—mothers and fathers who want their sons to be lawyers, sons who want their parents to pay more attention to them. If we'd just give up wanting people to do what we want them to do, we could all sit back and relax."

O'Malley paced back and forth on the porch. "Vlad, I'm really sick and tired of talking about psychopathic monsters who steal and kill children for a hobby. This one's too close to home. I want it to be all over and done with."

"You still want to know what happened, don't you?"

"Oh, for Christ's sake. Are you nuts? Of course, I do. Of course the parents do. Of course everybody does. Don't you?"

"Do you think the killer is still here in the village?"

"What do I have to say? Stop with the questions."

"Life's sometimes not pleasant, huh?"

"Sometimes it's not. I've got an idea. Let's go fishing. You can use Danny's gear. Got everything you need right here. Boots and everything. What do you say?"

"What took you so long to ask?"

"Oh, should we stop for cigarettes? You're out of those fancy Tareytons."

"No. Grab another pack of yours. I'll smoke yours."

"I was afraid of that."

"Ah, are those your fishing pajamas, or do you plan to change?"

31

" … We gotta go and never stop going till we get there."
"Where we going, man?"
"I don't know but we gotta go."
— From *On The Road* by Jack Kerouac

Vladimir backed the Jaguar out of the garage. It was ten in the morning. He drove down Glengary Road, took a right onto North Highland Avenue, and then a left onto Old Post Road. It was Monday. The commuters had caught their Manhattan-bound trains, and there was virtually no one on the streets when he turned into Rosone's Chrysler-Plymouth dealership. He parked in one of the spaces marked "Customers." The doors of the service bay were open. Two cars were up on the racks. Joe Rosone was standing under one of them talking to a mechanic. He was pointing up to something under the car.

Vladimir looked at them and went inside. There was no one in the showroom. He picked a brochure out of the rack by the door, paged through it, rolled it up, and stuffed it into his back pocket. There was a maroon four-door Plymouth Fury sedan on the showroom floor alongside a two-door copper and white one. He went over to the two-door model and, grasping his hands behind his back, bent over and peered inside.

"Hmmm," he thought, "white Naugahyde upholstery with light tan piping. Kinda like my Jag. Leather for the common man. Nice."

Rosone came up behind him, rubbing his hands, and shuffling his feet. He cleared his throat so as not so startle Vladimir.

Rosone wore a starched red-stripped spread-collar shirt, dark blue dress pants, and a pale blue tie with bright red elephants embroidered all over it. His shoulders were thick and broad, his chest big. The sleeves of the shirt were stretched tightly around his biceps. His gut, solid as a fully inflated Goodyear tire, hung slightly over his belt. He looked like a man who had once pumped iron but given it up. He snugged up his tie and rubbed his hands together again in the universal car-salesman manner.

"Good morning. Name's Rosone, Joe Rosone. Name's on the door. And your name?"

"Vladimir Petrovsky."

"Petrovsky. Well, Mr. Petrovsky … Oh, say, you're from the ballet school up on Glengary Road. Mrs. Petrovsky's ballet school.

"Yes."

"Shopping for a new car or a used one, Mr. Petrovsky? Either way you'll be glad you came to Rosone's."

"A new car."

"Alright, Mr. Petrovsky, have you got a trade in?"

"Yes."

"Got it with you."

"Right outside."

"Well, let's go out and have a look at it."

Both men walked out the door and Rosone's eyes widened when he saw the Jaguar.

"That yours, Mr. Petrovsky?

"Yes."

"Nice car. Don't think I've seen it around town." Rosone circled the car stroking his chin with his right hand, rubbing his belly with his left. Then he stopped, put his hand on the door handle, and turned his head toward Vladimir. "Mind if I look inside?"

"No, not at all."

Rosone opened the driver-side door and poked his head in, rotating it to look up at the ceiling, and then back down and around to look into the back seat. He ran his hand over the top of the front seat pausing to squeeze the leather. As he did this he stole a glance at the odometer. "Christ, look at that. This guy must have walked to church!" he thought.

Without removing his head from the car, he said, "Looks in nice shape, Mr. Petrovsky. That's for sure. Real nice shape. Real leather interior, too, no surprise; they call this color ... what, *café* something or other, right? *Café au lait*? That's it. And this sunroof. Don't see many of these. It's custom, right? Good job. Can I try it?" He reached up, paused and waited for Vladimir's approval.

"Sure, go ahead."

Rosone hooked his index finger in the chrome handle, twisted it and slid the panel back. It took only slight pressure to overcome inertia and start it rolling back and then the ball bearings took over and the panel slid into the pocket as smoothly and as quietly as a cat jumping on a couch. "Pretty slick," said Rosone. Oh, was he gonna make some money on this deal. "Well, let's go inside and look this puppy up in the Blue Book. He was thinking: "Three years old. The 3.8-liter S-type sedan. Six cylinders. Dual carbs. Disc brakes on all four wheels. What a beauty. Never taken a Jag in trade before but no problem."

Vladimir followed Rosone back inside, and they sat down in his office, a little three-walled cubicle set in the corner of the showroom.

Rosone put on his reading glasses, licked his thumb and began flicking through the pages of the Blue Book. Without looking up, he said "Got any particular model in mind? For your new car, I mean."

"A Plymouth."

Rosone laughed. "Well, you've come to the right place. Two door, four door, station wagon, convertible?"

"The one right there," said Vladimir pointing, "that copper and white one by the door."

"Oh, man. That's the Plymouth Sport Fury III. It's loaded. Got 375 horses and all the options—automatic transmission, power steering, white-wall tires, full chrome wheel covers, a stereo radio, white vinyl covered top, air-conditioning, little lights in the ashtrays and glove compartment. *The works!* Slickest car in the Plymouth line. Son, you got an eye for cars."

"Do they come with sunroofs?" Vladimir asked.

"Oh, afraid not. But, hey, this baby looks just like a convertible. The latest thing. That's the newest metallic paint. The very latest. See how it sparkles. What they do is grind up real copper and mix it right into the paint. Gives it that metallic effect. Very popular car. Sporty. Cops use the stripped down version. Yeah, the New York cops. Good choice." He looked down, copied something out of the Blue Book onto a pad of paper, swiveled in his chair, and put the Blue Book back on the shelf.

"I'll get the keys, and we'll take a little test drive. Gonna knock your socks off! Then we'll come back and review the numbers." Rosone rubbed his hands together, slid his chair back, and stood up.

"That won't be necessary. I've read the brochure," said Vladimir, knowing that he would miss the sunroof and thinking that a *faux* convertible with *faux* leather seats was really rather tacky. But he liked the way the car looked. Sort of art nouveau-ish in a postmodern way.

"You don't want to take a test drive?"

"No. Don't need to. And I'd like to get the car later today."

"Later today?"

"This afternoon. Is that's possible."

"I'll need time to do the paperwork, run the numbers, do the registration, plates, insurance. Oh, yeah, that car, the Sport Fury III, it's one of our demos. So it's actually ready for the road as she stands. What's more, 'cause of that, I can sweeten the deal. Save you some money. Just got her in. Got only a little over thirty miles on her. Heh, heh, not much more than your Jag." He laughed out loud at his joke and slapped his thigh. Won't take long to prep it. But it will take a little while, you know, to do the paper work."

"I understand. Tell me what you need."

"We need your registration, title, proof of insurance."

"All the papers are in the glove compartment. I have some errands to run. I'll stop back this afternoon. How about around three o'clock? Think you can have it ready by then?"

"Yeah, sure. Should be no problem. But, hey, we haven't talked numbers yet."

"I'd like to trade even."

"Even? Ah, let me figure that out. Can I have Angelo check out your Jag? Only take a second. While he's at it he can get the papers out of the glove compartment, too. That OK?"

"Sure."

"OK," he turned toward the service bay, "Hey, Angelo, come over here for a minute!"

The Jaguar was only three years old. It had a Goldie custom sunroof, the best of its kind, and chrome wire wheels. The wheels alone were worth $300 apiece. Angelo saw immediately that the car looked brand new. Rosone knew from the Blue Book price that he could trade even with Petrovsky and still make a nice profit. The Jaguar dealer across the Tappan Zee Bridge in Nyack would buy Petrovsky's car at the right price in a flash. For a little extra profit, he'd remove the wire wheels and sell them separately. Maybe even sell them to the same dealer in Nyack in a separate deal. He figured that's probably where they bought the car in the first place and probably had it serviced there, too. Hell, it had hardly been driven—couldn't have needed much service. But they'd have all the service records down there anyway.

"So, OK, not a problem," he thought, "why not tell Mr. Petrovsky that he could do the whole deal for, say, a thousand dollars? Tax, tags, the works. No, he'd do a straight trade. Still make plenty that way. Unusual, but no sense dickering; his Jag's a sweet car, a creampuff, and, besides, he's a local fellow, why complicate things? If he wants to trade for that Plymouth Fury III straight up, what the hell? Done deal. Hell, if I weren't a damn Plymouth dealer, I'd keep that 3.8 S-type Jag for myself, make it the family car."

Angelo came over and walked around the Jaguar, bending down to look at the tread on the Michelin tires. Then he stuck his head inside to check the odometer. He walked around to the passenger side, opened the door, and took the papers out of the glove compartment and put them beside him on the seat. Then he pulled the hood release, got out and opened it.

"Mind if I crank her?"

"Go ahead," said Vladimir. "Keys are in the ignition."

Angelo started her up and raced the engine a couple of times. "She roars like a lion, purrs like a pussy cat."

He rolled down the window and yelled: "Hey, boss, want me to give her a spin around the block?"

"Naw."

Angelo turned the ignition off and walked over to hand the papers to Rosone. "Looks good to go, boss."

"OK, Mr. Petrovsky. An even trade. See you this afternoon, around three. OK?" Rosone held the driver-side door open for Vladimir.

"Sure. Fine," said Vladimir slipping onto the leather seat.

He drove the Jaguar off the lot and into the upper village. He stopped at the First Federal Bank and withdrew ten thousand dollars from the joint Petrovsky account. He took a cashier's check for nine thousand dollars and asked the teller for the other thousand in cash—twenties and fifties. Then he drove back toward the train station and took the bypass south toward the Tappan Zee Bridge and Tarrytown.

In Tarrytown he parked in front of Gronstein's Hardware, one of those old-fashioned hardware stores that had been there for sixty years and still had the old, narrow-board oak floor that squeaked at every step. In the back, beyond the Sherman-Williams paint section, they had racks of work clothes: Carhart pants and jackets, Levi's jeans and jackets, and Timberlake work shoes.

Vladimir bought a Carhart jacket, a pair of Levis, a light blue cotton Western-style snap-front shirt, a pair of high-top boots and a pair of socks. The whole costume. He also bought a Polar-Tight picnic cooler.

He put the cooler in the back seat of the Jaguar. With the jeans and all stuffed into the Gronstein's shopping bag, he walked across Main Street to Gephart's drugstore where he bought a tube of Chap Stick, a Timex watch, a copy of the latest *U.S. News & World Report*, two packs of Camels, and a Bic lighter. He also bought a pack of manila envelopes and a roll of Scotch tape. At the cash register, he picked a folding pocketknife from the Schrade knife display and put that on the counter with the rest. He paid with a fifty and asked for singles and quarters in change. He tossed all his drugstore purchases on top of the clothes in the shopping bag.

On Main Street again, he paused to light a cigarette and then walked east past O'Riley's Tavern. The door was open and the smell of stale beer, tobacco smoke, and grease from the grill escaped into the street. Maybe he should stop in for a beer. But instead he walked on down the hill toward the river.

His destination was the launderette at the end of the street. It was open but deserted. He went in and plopped the shopping bag on a chair. With his new knife, he cut all the tags off his new jeans, jacket, and shirt. He picked a machine near the door and inserted some quarters into the soap slots and stuffed his new clothes into the washer.

He went back to the chair and pulled the shoebox out of the shopping bag, opened it, and removed the tissue paper. He reached in the bag again and got the roll of Scotch tape and one of the manila envelopes. He laid everything out on the Formica table opposite the row of washers and dryers. Then he took the Breitling off his wrist, looked at it for a brief nostalgic moment, then rolled it carefully in the tissue paper and stuffed in into the manila envelope. He folded the envelope over once and taped it on all sides. Then he dropped the package into the shopping bag.

While he waited for the wash cycle to finish, he sat down in the red vinyl and chrome chair by the door and paged through the *U.S. News & World Report*.

A skinny, middle-aged woman came in embracing a bundle of sheets and towels. She had short, black, unwashed hair, dirty fingernails, and she wore a black sleeveless T- shirt and tight ragged jeans shorts. She dropped her bundle on the floor in front of one of the washing machines, rubbed her face, smoothed her hair back, and scratched her ass.

By the time his new clothes were washed and dried it was high noon, according to his new Timex. He spread the clothes on the Formica table and smoothed them with the palm of his hand. The jeans and jacket looked OK, but the shirt was wrinkled. He looked in the back at the ironing board with the quarter-slotted iron sitting on top but thought the better of it. He had no idea how to iron a shirt.

The woman was looking at him and noticed his hesitation. Actually read his mind.

"Hey, fella, if you got the quarters for the iron, for a buck and a cigarette, I'd iron that shirt for ya. Hell, the jacket too. And touch up them jeans."

"OK, fine," he said and walked over to her. He handed her the shirt, the jacket, the jeans, three quarters, and a dollar bill.

"It's only a one-quarter job. Here, take these back."

She handed him two of the quarters. He offered her a cigarette.

"Camels? Jeez," she wrinkled up her face. "That's all ya got? I didn't think nobody smoked 'em no more. Camels, I mean. Nobody 'cept a soon-to-be cowboy like you. Ain't ya heard the warnings? Don't ya got a filter tip cigarette?"

"No," said Vladimir amused at the woman's directness.

"OK, beggars can't be choosers. That's what they say." She took the cigarette and said, "Got a light?"

Vladimir lit her cigarette with his new Bic and sat back down in the chair to read his magazine and wait for her to finish the ironing.

"Must be going on vacation, huh? Don't want to look like a dude with brand new jeans, huh? Don't ya got a woman ta do your washin' and ironin'?" She chuckled as she bent over the shirt. "Don't want to press them jeans, just shake 'em out. Don't want no crease in jeans. Not cool. But I can, you know, touch 'em up with the iron. And, hey, I'll press the jacket, too. Do that for another cigarette. Maybe another dollar. Is that a deal?"

"It's a deal. I owe you another cigarette and a dollar."

When she had finished, he folded everything neatly, put them back into the shopping bag. He bade farewell to the skinny lady in the launderette.

On his way back up the hill, he decided to stop in O'Riley's for a beer. There were three guys hunched over bottles of Budweiser and shots of whiskey at the end of the bar. They were dressed in jeans, T-shirts, and baseball caps. When he came in they turned their heads in unison like spectators at a tennis match. The closest one reached up and pushed his cap onto the back of his head to get a better view. O'Riley himself was behind the bar at the back. Without moving, he looked at Vladimir and said, "What'll you have, buddy?"

Vladimir thought for a moment, maybe a Martini. But that seemed out of place. "A beer, please."

"Bottle or draft?"

"Bottle."

"Brand?"

Vladimir looked at the beer bottles lined up behind the bar. Then he looked around at the neon signs. The biggest one said "Budweiser." So he said, "Budweiser."

O'Riley walked to the center of the bar and slid back the top of the cooler, pulled out a bottle of Bud, and toweled it off. He was an enormous man and, in his hand, with fingers like sausages, the beer bottle looked about as big as a family-sized tube of Pepsodent.

"One buck," he said as he set the bottle in front of Vladimir.

"May I have a glass, please?"

"Now what kind of a glass would ya be wantin', sir," said O'Riley playing to his still attentive audience of three.

"I don't know. Just a glass."

"What would ya be needin' a glass for, sonny boy?"

Vladimir sensed that he'd broken some unknown rule or custom. But he had no idea what it was. So he said, "For the beer, of course."

"For the beer, of course. Oh, *of course*. To drink the beer. Well, that's why I took the cap off. So's you could drink yur beer."

"I'd prefer a glass if you don't mind."

"Oh, I don't mind. No, not at all." O'Riley reached under the bar and produced a glass, a small highball glass. He picked up the bar towel and polished it with great ceremony, holding it up to the light , turning it from side to side before setting it down in front of Vladimir.

"Thank you."

"You're mightily welcome, son."

His last stop was the Tarrytown Post Office. He walked in with the manila-envelope package he'd wrapped at the launderette. He went over to one of the tables along the sidewall, picked up a pen, and printed a name and address on it. Then he took it to the window.

He didn't get back to Rosone's until three o'clock. Good timing. And, there, right out front, sat the metallic-copper, white vinyl-topped Plymouth. Angelo had Windexed the windows, gone over the inside with a Dirt Devil and rubbed down the outside with a chamois cloth. He even filled the tank.

Vladimir parked his Jaguar beside the new Plymouth and walked into the showroom. Rosone was sitting in his cubicle. As Vladimir approached, Rosone looked up.

"Hey, Mr. Petrovsky. There she is. Right outside. See her? Man in that car the girls will be crawling all over you. Ah, just need you to sign a few papers. Have a seat.

"Here's the deal, Mr. P. Even Steven. Straight trade. Just like you said. How's that sound? Your Jag for my Plymouth. Tax, tags, license, the works. Plus a full tank of gas with my compliments. Regular, always use regular. Got all the papers right here on the desk."

Vladimir signed the papers and handed Rosone the keys to the Jaguar. Rosone handed the Plymouth keys to Vladimir. They shook hands and walked out front together. Both were smiling.

Vladimir went over to the Jaguar for one last look. All his life he had been perfecting the art of forgetting, but today, when he touched the Jaguar and ran his fingers along the edge of the hood, memories fluttered up into his mind like a flock of pigeons in a park. Images, fleeting and out of focus, of the times he'd spent at Croton Point, at Croton Dam. He could see those scenes as if they were pictures in a photo album. Then, suddenly, darker images fluttered up like bats out of a cave. But the instant they appeared, he scattered them by the strong wind of his will, and they disappeared like vampires before a crucifix.

He opened the door of the Jaguar, pulled out the Gornstein shopping bag, and the cooler, and shut the door gently, savoring the familiar "thunk." He walked over to the new Plymouth, opened its driver-side door and swung the shopping bag inside. Did the same with the cooler. Then he slid behind the wheel.

He took a long, deep breath. He was surprised to discover that he actually enjoyed the new-car smell. He inhaled another helping of it, more slowly this time, savoring it. He wiggled his butt from side to side settling it into the *faux*-leather seat. He reached down with his left hand and pulled the seat-adjustment lever up. Then he pushed the seat back three notches. His ankle-high buckle boots fit the pedals nicely. "This was pretty easy," he thought, "Must be nothing unusual about trading a three-year-old Jaguar sedan for a brand-new Plymouth. He remembered Rosone's words, "Straight up. Even Steven." He reached over with his right hand and gave the seat a squeeze. "Nice," he thought, "but," mimicking the speech of the woman he'd met in the launderette, "Naugahyde ain't glove leather, baby." He inserted and turned the ignition key.

"Good luck, Mr. Petrovsky." Rosone waved. "Remember to have the car serviced right here. You know oil changes—get 'em every three to four thousand miles—and when you do, have the tires rotated. We do that free. Use special vinyl cleaner on the top. On the Naugahyde seats, too. We put a can in the glove compartment for you."

Vladimir rolled down the window. "Thank you," he said as he turned off the lot onto Old Post Road. Nice car, he thought. Really nice.

He turned left toward the railroad station and then right to get onto the by-pass. Then he headed North to Peekskill, then on to Beacon where he turned left, crossed the Hudson River and headed due West with his full tank of gas.

He felt an enormous sense of relief, anticipation, and excitement. First, he'd get rolling down the highway, and then he'd pull into a rest stop and change into his new clothes and head into his new life. What lay ahead was a beginning. What lay behind was the past and it wasn't worth remembering. There would be no memories. No regrets. His father, he imagined, would be proud of him for doing this. He'd walked out, too. He reached down and turned on the radio, set the FM station scanner, pressed the select button, and held it until he picked up a country music station. He was tired of Tchaikovsky and all that. The first voice he heard was Willie Nelson's. Of course, he didn't know who Willie was then, but he liked what he heard. The artlessness of the performance put an involuntary smile on his lips. The steady hum of the 375 under the hood kept that smile there for miles.

"Men?" she echoed. "I think there are six or seven of them in existence. I saw them, several years ago. But one never knows where to find them. The wind blows them away. They have no roots, and that makes their life very difficult."

— From the Kathryn Woods' translation of
The Little Prince, by Antoine de Saint-Exupery

The world he left, the world of Tchaikovsky and all that, was Mrs. Petrovsky's world. Not his. It was a balletic world that had come to Paris, London, and then New York directly from St. Petersburg and Moscow, blown like grains of pollen across the continent and then across the Atlantic by the bitter winds that rose in the aftermath of the Bolshevik Revolution. So powerful was this pollination that not long after its arrival in New York, the putative American ballet ceased to exist. Henceforth, ballet in New York, and, therefore, in America, if not everywhere else at the time, became Russian ballet. It was not long before the master of the dance in New York was the inestimable George Balanchine, who ruled the New York barre from 1933 to 1983, thus making New York the epicenter of the world of classical dance—a rare, exotic, intensely sensual Russified world where even the men wore mascara, pink tights, and lilac perfume.

163

Mrs. Petrovsky's mother brought this world and her daughter to America from Russia. And soon, no, instantly, ballet and Balanchine were the center of both mother and daughter's life. For the mother, it was the achievement of a childhood dream. For the daughter, it was like living in a childhood dream. A dream that would end twenty years latter and thirty-three miles up the river from Manhattan in the quaint, little village of Croton-on-Hudson, New York.

Over those twenty years Mrs. Petrovsky would go from being the prima ballerina—the artistic mistress of Balanchine's muse—to being the aging mistress of a suburban ballet school where coltish young darlings and their plump, awkwardly earnest mothers came to lay their own balletomane dreams at her feet.

The adjustment was obviously not easy for her. In her day she had been the chosen one. The one Balanchine had chosen himself. Yes, the great man had singled her out at the age of eighteen, coddled and coached her with the warm, seductive yet imperial aloofness of a crown prince. Often, in his company, her cheeks would redden when she realized that his touch was not entirely the innocent kind. She worshipped him. He, she was sure because he gave every sign—albeit princely and subtle—worshipped her too. Always would.

Then one day it was over.

He would pass her in the hallway without so much as a word, not even a glance or a pause. After having been the glittering angel on the tip-top of his tree, she had now become invisible. Once the chosen one, now the unseen, unacknowledged, and forgotten one.

What explanation was there for his sudden coldness? Everyone knew the answer, including Mrs. Petrovsky herself. Balanchine had chosen his next protégé, a resplendently young and talented ballerina. In this new protégé's unspoiled face, she saw the past glory of her own childhood, the freshness of her own youth, and everywhere she looked, it seemed, were reminders of all her early years. Suddenly there was youth and beauty everywhere.

In those years, Ashton's *The Dream*, a balletic retelling of Shakespeare's *A Midsummer Night's Dream*, was enjoying great popularity. In Shakespeare's play, Puck had a magic juice that would make one whose eyelids were anointed with it fall in love with the first person seen upon awakening. Balanchine's eyelids had always been anointed with this juice. Being surrounded by youth and beauty, he immediately fell in love with youth and beauty. In his case, however, the magic juice did not confer fidelity to the first person seen. He was a serial lover.

The drift of her life, she thought, was like a fugue, a pattern repeated again and again: First a fickle impresario, next an unfaithful husband— both anointed with Puck's magic juice, infatuated with youth and beauty (and who is not?)—and now Vladimir was gone. She saw the pattern repeating itself in her life. Deserted by her own dear son and singular passion, the only meaningful thing left in her life. Now, he, too, had been anointed with Puck's magic juice and was in love with youth and beauty. That damned duo: first Constance and then Ellen had swept her, like so much dust, out of his mind ... and heart.

Vladimir, as her husband and Balanchine before him, had fallen out of love with her. They were all serial lovers. All the men in her life. First, for Vladimir, her son, it would be one favorite girl and then another. Those tender little girls. Where was their innocence? They had none; they were fully bloomed bitches at the age of eleven. Some earlier. They knew the game they were playing. They played it, oh, so well. They knew what she knew, that all men carry Puck's anointment on their eyelids.

Vladimir had been away at boarding school and then college. So, before his joining her at the ballet school, she had no knowledge of any of his other flirtations. She hadn't really thought about that. And, at first, when she became aware of his attraction to Constance, she found it somewhat amusing. Certainly not threating. Nothing more than a harmless attraction. Indeed, a polite affectation on his part. He was just doing his job. As time went on, however, she began to perceive it in a more sinister light. Of course she realized that it was she who had created and then fed his desire for the company of these pretty little flowers. But how could she help it? This was all that was left of her world. The only thing she knew. After all she was the mistress of a ballet school for young girls. She herself was surrounded by them. But, in the case of her son, she never imagined that an attraction to them would develop. Was she really such a fool?

Had those little conspirators become serious competition for his love for her, his own mother? How could that be? They were girls, mere children. Was her son being drawn away from the Queen Bee by the sweet fragrance of these flowers?

"What moves me so deeply about this Little Prince ... is his loyalty to a flower—the image of a rose that shines through his whole being like the flame of a lamp, even when he is asleep ... ."

— From the Kathryn Woods' translation of
The Little Prince, by Antoine de Saint-Exupery

Perhaps, she thought, she should close the school immediately. But how could she do that? The school was the last tie she had to her old world, her old glory. How painful leaving that would be. How impossible. How empty and meaningless such a life would be. She could not imagine a life without Vladimir; he was her son. Perhaps, if he were to come back, they could go to Europe together, sell the mansion, and buy another home, a cottage outside Paris. But no matter where they went, she knew in the depths of her heart that he would one day find and follow the scent of youth and beauty.

Damn those girls. Damn their flirtatious ways. Little bitches. Soft little kittens with sharp claws. Temptresses. It was their fault, not his.

Gone he was. Gone without a word. Would he be gone forever. No, *please*, not forever.

It's that time when the pull of the blue highway is strongest,
when the open road is a beckoning, a strangeness, a place
where a man can lose himself.
    — From *Blue Highways* by William Least Heat Moon

O'Malley was in his kitchen in his old slippers and bathrobe making coffee. The river flowed outside, full to the tops of its banks. Nothing much to do but fix the coffee and check the mail. He'd already read the paper.

The porch was slippery with dew, and he walked carefully, sliding his feet forward until he could hold onto the railing. The sidewalk was not as slippery as the porch; walking there was easier. He kicked aside the rake and shovel. He pulled down the handle of the mailbox and reached inside. The usual stuff: bills and junk mail. Then he felt a fat envelope, a manila envelope folded over, Scotch-taped, and stuffed with what felt like a wad of paper. He squeezed it. There was something hard and heavy inside. "What th' hell is this?"

His name and address were printed on the envelope in neat block letters. No return address. He picked up the pile of mail, and the little package, and went back inside. He'd need a penknife to slice it open.

Like angels that have monster eyes
Over your bedside I shall rise ....
— From "The Ghost," *Flowers of Evil*
by Charles Baudelaire

Almost no one in Croton, yes, even the mothers who took their daughters to the Petrovsky School of Classical Ballet, really knew Vladimir in any meaningful way. Those who did "know" him knew him only in the most casual way. It's true, he was an interesting guy, and when gone, he left hardly a mark on the wall of their consciousness. In fact surprisingly few people in town who had bothered to take any notice of them—including some of the mothers—actually even knew that the Petrovsky's were mother and son. All the others thought, if they thought about it at all, that they were just that odd, rather eccentric couple that lived in the old Fundeburk mansion on Glengary Road. So when Vladimir left, few people really noticed, much less cared, that he was gone. No one missed him in the sense of having a significant portion of his or her lives altered by his leaving. The girls at the school? Not really. There were always too many other things to do. Other amusements.

Joe Rosone had, however, called Corsetti to tell him about Vladimir trading in the Jaguar on a new Plymouth. "Thought you might be interested," he said. Corsetti also knew about the bank withdrawal. The vice president at First Federal, Paul Cowley, had called him, too. Cowley had no idea that the ten thousand dollars was travel money and knew nothing about the Plymouth deal, but he, too, thought it prudent to call Corsetti. "Thought you guys down there ought to know."

At first, of course, his leaving—his disappearance—aroused suspicions. Everyone who thought about it for a moment knew that standard abduction investigation protocol had placed him at the top of the suspect list. That's why the calls were made. Rosone and Cowley were aware of that. But there was not one shred of credible evidence to tie Vladimir Petrovsky to the disappearance of either Constance or Ellen. Only ugly rumors.

There was nothing Corsetti could do about Vladimir's leaving. He was not a suspect in any actionable sense. *Yes*, he was odd, eccentric, played with girls, knew them—he had the profile of a "queer duck" and all the opportunity—but, damn it, there was not one item of physical evidence, not one witness, nothing to implicate him in any way. That Jaguar was in Vladimir's name alone. The bank account was held jointly. No irregularities. When told of the transactions, Mrs. Petrovsky made no complaint.

When asked, she said that she did not want to talk about it. It was a personal matter. Vladimir had just wanted a different car, a new car. So he had bought one. He had gone for a drive in it. Taken a short trip. That's all. A vacation. A change of scene. No, she did not know where, exactly. He's a grown man. Yes, truthfully, it was somewhat unexpected. Yes, that's true. But he is a strong-willed young man, and they sometimes do unexpected things.

Of course, after each of the girl's disappearance, Vladimir was a suspect just as, say, a coach would be a suspect if one of his athletes disappeared. Yet, as far as Vladimir was concerned, no girl enrolled at the school, not Constance before she disappeared, not Ellen before she disappeared, had ever complained about any thing inappropriate in his conduct toward them. Indeed, all the ballerinas said they felt that he never really played favorites. "He was nice to us all," they said. In short, none of them, and no one else for that matter, said anything that would have made Vladimir anything more than a routine, let's say "circumstantial," suspect.

No witness in either of the disappearances existed.

Every single one of the ballerinas' mothers, including Mrs. Carmichael and Mrs. Sheffield, thought Vladimir was indeed a positive influence on their children. He was a clean-cut young man, clearly not a child molester, let alone a hideous murderer. He simply did his job at the school as professionally as one might expect.

The enduring consensus was, therefore, that what happened was the act of a mysterious stranger. It was no one's fault that some monster had come into town and stolen two little girls. For goodness sakes, it had been over four years since little Constance disappeared. Yes, lightening did strike twice. That's true. But that makes it all the more improbable that it would ever strike again. It was best for them to forget all the unpleasantness, to get on with their lives.

Needless to say, the real estate people, they wanted to see the memory of the two disappearances fade sooner rather than later: "For God's sake, let's get on with our lives and stop this morbid preoccupation with the unspeakable and the unexplainable. It has nothing to do with us. In a few more years we'll have forgotten about it completely. Just you wait and see. That's the way the world works."

But, of course, for some, there was no forgetting, not in a few years, not in a lifetime. For the Carmichaels and the Sheffields it would be forever. In a few more years both families moved out of the village. There were too many memories. They would endeavor to take the good ones with them and leave the bad ones behind.

Mrs. Carmichael had a very hard time of it. She didn't want to leave town. She believed that Constance would return someday. She truly believed that. She wanted everything to remain the same. To change anything would be an admission that she had given up hope. But eventually her husband persuaded her that it would be best for them to go somewhere else. So they left.

Mrs. Sheffield never recovered; mothers never really do. Nor do fathers. She became aloof, then reclusive, moody, and clinically depressed. She and her husband were divorced five years after Ellen's disappearance, and after that her life, they say, disintegrated entirely. There are whispers that she is upstate in an asylum. Paul Sheffield was remarried.

Corsetti retired and moved to Pensacola, Florida.

Out in Big Sky Country, in Bozeman, Montana, there was a new florist in town, a nice, well-spoken young man, a fly fisherman and a country music fan. Keeps to himself mostly. The few who know him find nothing particularly odd or peculiar about him—except that he drinks his beer out of a glass. But then what would you expect, he's an Easterner.

As the years passed, there was really no one left in Croton to care anymore. Not about the girls, let alone Vladimir.

36

Dear as remembered kisses after death
So sad, so strange, the days that are no more.
— From *Tears, Idle Tears*
by Alfred Lord Tennyson

After Vladimir hit the highway, Mrs. Petrovsky continued to run the ballet school for a few years, but there was no one to help her with the schedule book, there was no dance master, and each year she grew increasingly preoccupied with the memory of Vladimir and the intense pain of having lost him. She had, after all, done everything she could to keep him. Now, without him her life had become absolutely, utterly empty; her whole life was now contained in the petty routines of each day, each day the same. A fugue of pain, isolation, and loneliness.

She could not believe that Vladimir had abandoned her. She could not believe that he would never return. She wandered around the mansion expecting to see Vladimir, maybe in the kitchen or out in the garden. She'd stop and listen for his footsteps coming down the stairs in those calfskin ankle boots. She wept at every thought of him. She went up to his bedroom several times a day. She put fresh flowers on his bedside table. Every morning after her bath, she would go there and crawl, stomach down, on his bed, lie there naked, trying to absorb whatever remnant of him might be left there. She would submerge her nose in his pillow until it flattened like a child's nose pressed against a windowpane. She would claw at the sheets and press her breasts into them until her nipples reddened and ached.

"God, God, God, God, oh, God don't do this to me. Give me back my son. Why have you taken him away from me? Is this my punishment for loving him? Why am I being punished? It cannot have been wrong to love my son. He was my *only* son. My *only* child. Loving him as I did was not wrong. It is *not* wrong. It *was* not wrong. Give him back to me. Give him back to me. I will do anything if you will give him back to me."

Her anguish was immeasurable. Inconsolable. She would lie there spread eagled like an animal skin nailed to a trapper's drying board salted by her own tears, all hope now slain by a sword of despair thrust through her heart.

She was utterly abandoned. Not the strongest analgesic, not the brightest, sweetest bluebird, jonquil day could assuage the darkness, the brittle bitterness, the vast isolation and desolation she felt.

She would fall asleep spread there, exhausted from her weeping, the pillow wet with tears.

He was all she had. He was her world. When she died, it would be he and he alone who would grieve her loss; only he would be there to stand beside her grave and then depart to mourn her ceaselessly for a lifetime.

Now that he was gone, there would be no one there. He wouldn't even know. Would never know and never care. Her few friends had fallen from her life like late autumn leaves. She attended no church, professed no religion, and had no confidants. In Croton or anywhere else.

Time and again, wandering around in the mansion with all the curtains drawn; she would imagine that bleakest of scenes: A black casket hovering over a black hole dug in the wet earth on a grassless slope beside a leafless oak with rain slanting out of a gray late autumn or early winter sky. No flowers. No priest. No prayers. No mourners. No son. No husband. No one left to care.

And so it was, in the cemetery above the village, above the wide

Hudson on a day just as cold, wet, and gray and just as lonely as she had so many times imagined; Mrs. Petrovsky took her final journey … alone, save for two grave diggers leaning on their shovels and one solitary figure leaning against a nearby oak. He wore a plastic raincoat and a gray fedora, a dark blue suit, a black tie, white shirt, and black wingtip shoes.

As the gravediggers set aside their shovels and lowered the casket, he blessed himself with a gloveless hand. "In the name of the Father, and the Son, and the Holy Ghost." Then he raised his left hand to wipe the drops of rain from his face. As he did so, raindrops fell like tears on the face of his large stainless steel watch.

Down in the village, the old Funderburk mansion stood glistening greyly in the rain.

The End